BOOK FIVE

# SMOKED

USA TODAY BESTSELLING AUTHOR

## HEATHER SLADE

smoked

/smohkd/

*verb*

to smolder, burn, singe

# MORE FROM AUTHOR HEATHER SLADE

BUTLER RANCH
*Kade's Worth*
*Brodie's Promise*
*Maddox's Truce*
*Naughton's Secret*
*Mercer's Vow*
*Kade's Return*
*Butler Ranch Christmas*

WICKED WINEMAKERS
FIRST LABEL
*Brix's Bid*
*Ridge's Release*
*Press' Passion*
*Zin's Sins*
*Tryst's Temptation*

WICKED WINEMAKERS
SECOND LABEL
*Beau's Beloved*
Coming Soon:
*Cru's Crush*
*Bones' Bliss*
*Snapper's Seduction*
*Kick's Kiss*

ROARING FORK RANCH
Coming Soon:
*Roaring Fork Wrangler*
*Roaring Fork Roughstock*
*Roaring Fork Rockstar*
*Roaring Fork Rooker*
*Roaring Fork Bridger*

THE ROYAL AGENTS
OF MI6
*Make Me Shiver*
*Drive Me Wilder*
*Feel My Pinch*
*Chase My Shadow*
*Find My Angel*

K19 SECURITY
SOLUTIONS TEAM ONE
*Razor's Edge*
*Gunner's Redemption*
*Mistletoe's Magic*
*Mantis' Desire*
*Dutch's Salvation*

K19 SECURITY
SOLUTIONS TEAM TWO
*Striker's Choice*
*Monk's Fire*
*Halo's Oath*
*Tackle's Honor*
*Onyx's Awakening*

K19 SHADOW OPERATIONS
TEAM ONE
*Code Name: Ranger*
*Code Name: Diesel*
*Code Name: Wasp*
*Code Name: Cowboy*
*Code Name: Mayhem*

K19 ALLIED INTELLIGENCE
TEAM ONE
*Code Name: Ares*
*Code Name: Cayman*
*Code Name: Poseidon*
*Code Name: Zeppelin*
*Code Name: Magnet*

K19 ALLIED INTELLIGENCE
TEAM TWO
Coming Soon:
*Code Name: Puck*
*Code Name: Michelangelo*
*Code Name: Typhon*
*Code Name: Hornet*
*Code Name: Reaper*

PROTECTORS
UNDERCOVER
*Undercover Agent*
*Undercover Emissary*
Coming Soon:
*Undercover Savior*
*Undercover Infidel*
*Undercover Assassin*

THE INVINCIBLES
TEAM ONE
*Decked*
*Edged*
*Grinded*
*Riled*
*Smoked*

THE INVINCIBLES
TEAM TWO
*Bucked*
*Irished*
*Sainted*
*Hammered*
*Ripped*

THE UNSTOPPABLES
TEAM ONE
*Furied*
*Merried*

COWBOYS OF
CRESTED BUTTE
*A Cowboy Falls*
*A Cowboy's Dance*
*A Cowboy's Kiss*
*A Cowboy Stays*
*A Cowboy Wins*

# Table of Contents

# Prologue

*Smoke*

*"Siren!"* I called out as I ran into the burnt-out building I'd seen her enter a few seconds before I did. *"Siobhan! Where the fuck are you?"*

I knew why she'd run past the fire marshal and into the scorched shell of the former antique shop: she was looking for the safe that was in the back storage room of the derelict place. I also knew why sh e refused to answer me.

*"Siren!"* I yelled again, staying low to the ground, hoping to get a glimpse of her through the haze of smoke.

As if it were a special effect, the cloud suddenly cleared, and in front of me stood the woman I'd hated and loved equally in the months I'd known her.

*"Get out of here, Smoke. This is none of your con-cern,"* she shouted.

"It may not be," I said, taking a step in her direction. "But you are. Let me help you, Siobhan."

"I was never your concern, *Broderick,* except to play with." Her Irish brogue was thick, like when she was about to cry.

"Please." I took another step closer and held out my hand. Before I was near enough for her to take it, I heard a crack above us. I dove in her direction, covering her body with mine as the still-smoldering ceiling came crashing down on us both.

# Part 1

*Two Months Earlier*

# 1

*Smoke*

I held my breath when the doctor came out of the double doors with a grim look on his face.

"Siobhan Gallagher's family," the nurse with him called out. I stood and walked toward them.

"That's me."

"Your name?"

"Broderick Torcher."

The doctor cleared his throat. "The surgery was successful, and Ms. Gallagher is in stable condition."

I let out the breath I'd been holding, sensing there was a "but" coming. Sure enough, his next sentence confirmed it.

"There was brain trauma associated with her injuries…"

I felt the bile rising in my throat.

"Ms. Gallagher has suffered a series of small strokes. Some movement may have been affected, as well as her memory."

"What do you mean by 'affected'?"

"As with any stroke, when the patient first regains consciousness, the symptoms are typically at their worst. Some regain full physical and mental capacity immediately. Others, it takes longer."

"What, *specifically,* has been affected?"

"We don't know fully as she's only regained consciousness intermittently."

I took another deep breath, restraining myself from grabbing the man by the throat, putting his back to the wall, and insisting he answer my fucking question. Instead, I spoke slowly. "For the third time, what…did…you…mean…by…affected?"

"Ms. Gallagher was having difficulty controlling movement on the left side of her body. We expect this to improve relatively quickly."

"You said physical and mental."

"The patient was experiencing confusion—"

My patience was gone. "What kind of confusion?" I growled at the man.

"As I said, for now, much of her condition is unknown."

"You're not answering my questions." I was trained to recognize when people were hiding something, and this man sure as shit was. If this doc thought he could get anything over on me, he was in for a rude awaken-ing when he experienced my ire in full force.

"It would be premature to give you any definitive answers regarding her symptoms."

I rubbed the back of my neck, wishing I could turn around, walk out of the hospital, and never look back.

"What is the nature of your relationship with Ms. Gallagher?" he asked.

"Work colleagues."

The doctor raised his brow and looked at the nurse, who opened the folder she had in her hand and shuffled through the papers inside. She gave him a sheet containing the information I assumed he was looking for.

"You're listed as having her medical power of attorney."

"That's right." The reason why was none of his business.

"It's unlikely she'll remember you."

*"Excuse me?"*

"As I said, Ms. Gallagher has only regained consciousness for short amounts of time."

"And yet you predict she won't remember me?"

"We have reason to believe her memory has been affected." He studied me for a moment. "Do you have any other questions?"

A thousand, at least, but his track record at answering any I'd asked so far was zilch. I shook my head.

"You may see her now. If you'd like, the nurse can escort you to her room."

If I'd like? There's nothing I'd *like* less. However, this wasn't something I could walk away from. Siren wasn't someone I could walk away from.

The nurse waved her arm for me to follow.

"Hold up," I said, motioning to where I left a book and a cup of coffee near where I'd been sitting.

She folded her arms and drummed the fingers of one hand. I'd been sitting here for seven hours, waiting for some kind of word on Siren's condition. She could damn well wait for me to throw away a coffee cup.

I followed her behind the double doors and down a corridor.

"As you were informed, she's been awake on and off." The nurse stopped walking and cleared her throat. "I'll warn you that Ms. Gallagher's appearance may be somewhat alarming."

I didn't bother to tell the nurse that I'd seen things exponentially worse than alarming. *Horrific. Nightmarish. Gruesome.* Those were appropriately descriptive adjectives of the carnage I'd witnessed. Many of the scenes, I'd caused. A tiny woman lying in a hospital bed was the last thing that would *alarm* me.

Or so I thought. The woman who'd infuriated me like no other ever, sent my blood pressure skyrocketing with her inability to follow simple directives, and caused me to consider strangling her on countless occasions, looked like a broken doll lying on the gurney.

Her skin, already pale as alabaster, was ghostly white save for the purple bruises that marred its otherwise flawlessness. Beneath the edges of the thick bandages covering most of her scalp, I could see that her long inky-black hair had been shaved. The worst of what I saw, were the straps tying her arms to the bed's rails. I lifted the sheet and saw the same with her legs.

"Is this really necessary?" I slowly turned when the nurse cleared her throat but didn't answer. "What?"

"I'm sorry, Mister…"

"Torcher."

"Right. You have five minutes, after which, I'll need to accompany you back out to the waiting area."

I shook my head and looked back at Siren. "I'm not leaving."

"But you can't remain—"

"Watch me." I seethed, looking over my shoulder at the woman who was half my height and probably a quarter of my weight.

"Well, I suppose that since you have Ms. Gallagher's power of attorney, you would be considered her next of kin."

When she left, closing the door behind her, I pulled a chair closer to the bedside. I untied the bindings and studied Siren's features in a way I couldn't when she was awake. She'd never kept her devil tongue still enough for me to take my time appreciating her true beauty.

Like her hair, her lush eyelashes were black, as were her thin eyebrows that I'd seen more often raised in annoyance with me rather than at rest like they were now. Her angular cheekbones were pronounced on her oval face, more than her button nose, lush mouth, and soft chin.

Her appearance was similar to the photos I'd seen of my own grandmother, Nanna Ryan, when she was in her mid-twenties like Siren was.

You would think that two people who'd spent as much time together as Siren and I, would've talked about our families, but we hadn't.

I'd never said, but like her, my mother's family was Irish. Maeve Ryan-Torcher's family hailed from Kinsale in County Cork, only sixteen miles south of the city bearing the same name as the county. The port and fishing village was best known for the hard-drinking yachtsmen and fishermen who spent whatever time they had off the water, on the nearby golf courses.

I'd visited a few times with my grandmother, the last of which was only a month before she passed away.

I knew from the background report I'd received on Siren from both the CIA and the Invincibles, the private intelligence firm she and I had accepted our last mission from, that her mother died when Siren was a teenager. There was no name listed as her father on her birth certificate.

In the same way I'd never been able to sit and stare at Siren's exquisite face, any perusal of her body I'd done was only when she wasn't looking. She was a wisp of a thing but with boobs that made everything she wore look sexy as fuck, even the cotton hospital gown.

When she shifted and groaned, I looked up into her wide-set Arctic-blue eyes.

"Smoke." Her voice was soft but made gravelly by the since-removed intubation tube required during her surgery.

"Siren," I murmured, stunned when she looked at the palm of her delicate hand as if she was reaching out to me.

"Closer," she wheezed.

"Don't try to talk," I said, scooting the chair forward.

Her eyes surveyed the room, and she looked at me questioningly.

"You're in Fernwood Hospital, about an hour outside London. Do you remember anything that happened?"

"No."

"You were shot during an op. You're lucky to be alive."

Her eyes opened wide. "An op?"

"We were on Konstantine von Habsburg's detail at Broadmoor Hospital."

Siren sunk deeper into the pillow, her brow furrowed. "Detail?"

Admittedly, I'd rarely heard the woman's voice be so subdued, unless she was speaking to someone other than me, but its frailty was worrisome. I remembered the doctor saying Siren's memory might have been affected by the series of strokes she'd suffered, but she clearly knew me.

"What's the last thing you recall?"

She shook her head and closed her eyes. "The island," she whispered.

The island? I clenched the fist she couldn't see and willed my body not to react in any other way. Of everything she might have said, that was the last thing I expected. I barely recalled it myself, not only because I'd pushed it out of my thoughts so many times, but also because of the rum-induced haze I'd been in on the one night when the heated passion between us turned from hate to lust.

Siren looked down at her open palm a second time and then up at me. "Smoke?"

I leaned forward and stroked the area around the place where the intravenous line was taped against her skin. *"Siren..."*

"Please," she whispered.

"What?"

"Hold me."

If she were any more alert, I would call her out for fucking with me, but the longing I saw in her eyes was too sincere.

I stood, trying to figure out a way to get my six-feet-five, two-hundred-and-sixty-pound frame positioned in such a way that I could put my arms around her without ripping out her IV or crushing her.

When she scooted her body over, the sheet moved with her. I could see her hospital gown had ridden up, exposing her bare hip. I grabbed the bedclothes and covered her before reaching down to give her an awkward hug.

"Lie with me."

It popped into my head again that Siren was playing me, but after one look into her imploring eyes, I rested my hip on the bed. "Be careful," I warned when she tried to scoot over a second time. I gingerly put one arm around her waist and folded the other above her head. She closed her eyes.

A few minutes later, the door opened and a different nurse scowled at me. Before she could speak, I eased away from the sleeping Siren, put my finger to my lips, and stood. I brushed past her and out the door when my cell phone rang with a call from the man who'd hired me to do a job I failed.

"Rile," I answered, leaning against the tiled wall of the corridor.

"How is Siren?"

"Out of surgery."

"And?"

I shrugged my shoulder, not that he could see me. "Stable," I muttered, trying to recollect the thoughts I'd been able to formulate before Siren's request to hold her caused my mind to go blank. "Rile, I—"

"Say no more. Your first duty is to your partner."

"But, Konstantine—"

"Is dead," he said, interrupting me for the second time.

"Kensington?" I asked of the woman we'd been hired to protect from a Hungarian madman. The Hungarian madman I'd let escape after he shot and almost killed Siren.

"She is safe and asleep at my side."

"I'm sorry, Rile." I got the words I'd wanted to say at the beginning of our conversation out.

"I'll notify Director Hughes of Siren's condition."

"Listen, can you keep the details vague for the time being?" If the Director of Irish Military Intelligence found out Siren had suffered several mini-strokes and her memory was sketchy at best, not to mention what the doctor had said about her having trouble controlling movement on the left side of her body, the likelihood of her ever being able to return to duty was minuscule.

"Of course, my friend, given I have none."

I could envision Rile's smirk. "For now, she's out of surgery and her condition is stable. That's all Hughes needs to know."

"Very well. We will speak again soon."

I stuffed my phone back in my pocket, wishing I could get my hands on a shot of bourbon before I went back into Siren's room. With that thought, the door opened and the nurse stepped out.

"She's asking for you."

# 2

*Siren*

"Where is Smoke?" I asked when I opened my eyes and felt a cold hand on my wrist.

"Smoke?" asked the woman who was attaching a blood-pressure cuff to my upper arm.

"The man who was here earlier."

"He stepped out."

"Did he say when he was coming back?"

"Shh." She glared at me while she pumped the ball, tightening the cuff. "Where in Ireland are you from?" she asked as she released it and typed something into her laptop.

"Um…" I scrunched my eyebrows. The name of my birthplace was right on the tip of my tongue, as they say, yet I couldn't recall it. Just like I couldn't recall much of anything else. I knew my name. And Smoke's.

Wait. His name couldn't just be Smoke. Like I couldn't recall where I hailed from, I couldn't remember his full name.

I rested my head against the pillow and closed my eyes. I opened them again when the woman's cold fingers rested on my pulse.

"What is that?" I asked as she inserted a needle in the port of my IV.

"Your pain medicine."

A warm sensation flooded into my arm and up through my chest. Why could I remember things like what an IV was called and even a port, but not the name of the place where I was born or the full name of the man I loved? I tried to fight against falling asleep before he came back, but was overcome by grogginess.

"Smoke…" I whispered.

When I woke, he was sitting in the chair beside me, studying something on his phone. His brow was furrowed. Did he do that often? Why couldn't I remember?

Every time I closed my eyes, I saw one thing. Smoke, holding himself above me as I lay on a blanket on the beach. Somehow, I knew we were on an island. It was nearly dark, but I could see his face, his eyes. I could remember every detail of his lips on mine and everything that followed. It wasn't just the memory of how our bodies felt, naked as the ocean breeze swept over us. It was more that I could recall every feeling I had from the first kiss until we lay in each other's arms by the light of the moon and stars. In the face of not remembering anything else, I knew deep in my soul that I loved Smoke and he loved me.

I opened my eyes a second time and found him studying me instead of his phone.

"How are you feeling?" he asked.

"Drugged."

He smiled. Or maybe he smirked.

"What?"

He leaned forward and rested his arms on his knees. "You aren't usually quite so…docile."

*"Docile?"* I might've shrieked if my throat didn't hurt so bad.

He laughed out loud. "There's the Siren I know."

I rested my head against the pillow. "There are so many things I can't remember. In fact, I remember almost nothing. The nurse asked where I was from in Ireland, and I couldn't tell her. I know your name is Smoke, but I don't know if that's your real name or your last name."

"My name is Broderick Torcher, and my code name is Smoke."

"Thank you." I sighed. "Wait. Code name?"

"I work in the intelligence business. So do you."

My head throbbed. "My name is Siobhan."

"That's right."

"Gallagher. Siobhan Gallagher."

"And your code name is Siren."

"Siren," I whispered. "Smoke and Siren."

"Hard to believe, but it was a coincidence. We both had our code names long before the first op we worked together."

"How long ago was that?"

He held up one finger when his phone vibrated. "I need to take this." He stood and walked out of the room.

I had so many questions. He said we had our code names before we worked together. Did we work for the same company?

The door opened, and instead of Smoke, a different nurse came in. I rested my head and closed my eyes when, like the other, she checked my blood pressure. I looked up at her when I felt her hand on my wrist.

"Wait, is that pain medicine?"

"It is," she said without even looking at me.

I tried to jerk my hand away, but it wouldn't budge. "Hang on."

"What?" she snapped.

"Another nurse already gave me pain medicine."

With the syringe still in hand, she picked up a piece of paper. "You're due. Once every four hours."

"I don't need it."

"Yeah, you do," said Smoke, coming in the door. "You're nowhere near ready to be off that stuff."

"How do you know?"

"If you had a mirror to look into, you'd know."

"What does that mean?"

Despite my protests, I felt the warm sensation flow through my arm and into my chest. *"Fecking hell,"* I groaned. "I don't want to sleep."

The bitch of a nurse scurried out, leaving Smoke smiling at me.

*"What?"*

"You'll be back to your regular self in no time."

If I could lift my arm, I'd have flipped him off, but I couldn't. Maybe the pain killers they kept shooting into it made it numb. "I wonder if that's a good thing," I muttered.

"You need to get some sleep, and I need to eat. I'll come back in the morning."

"Morning? What time is it now?"

"Almost midnight."

"You get calls on your mobile at midnight?"

"In our line of work, we get 'em twenty-four seven."

"Okay, well, goodnight, then."

"I'll see you tomorrow."

"Smoke, wait," I said when he turned to walk out. "You aren't going to kiss me goodnight?"

"Um…sure." He walked closer, leaned down, and kissed my forehead.

"You call that a kiss?"

His face was still close to mine, and he scrunched his eyes. I pursed my lips, and he brushed them with his.

"Better than nothing, I guess."

He stood and turned toward the door. "Yep, back to yourself in no time."

# 3



"What are you doin' up this late, old man?"

"Fuck you, Hammer. you're older than I am, and it's midnight."

"I'm older than you by a week, asshole. Hey, how's Siren?"

"That's what I'm calling about."

"Who."

"Siren."

"Right. She's not a that; she's a who."

"Jesus Christ, why did I call you?"

"Because you wanted to talk about Siren."

I looked longingly across the street at the pub that was already closed.

"Smoke? You there?"

"Yeah. I'm here. I need a drink."

"That bad?"

"Worse. A lot worse."

"Are we gonna play this two-, three-word game all night, or are ya gonna tell me somethin'?"

"She has amnesia."

"You're kidding."

He said it in such a way, I knew he didn't think I was. The other thing I knew, was that Hammer wouldn't tell a soul anything I said in this conversation. He was a lawyer. My lawyer. Actually, he was the lawyer for everyone who worked for the Invincibles. Not that what I was about to tell him counted as attorney-client privilege.

"Smoke?"

"Yeah, I'm here." I sat down on a bench outside my hotel. "She doesn't remember much of anything. Not even where she was born."

"But?"

"Fuck," I muttered under my breath. "We were both given a job by Rile DeLéon. Asset protection. He teamed us up."

"I know about the op, Smoke. What happened?"

"We were off duty one of the nights that we were on the island—"

"And?"

"If you'd shut up for a minute, I'd tell you." I waited. "Anyway, one thing led to another, and we had…sex."

*Crickets.*

"Hammer?"

"I'm here."

"That's what she remembers."

When he started to laugh and then kept laughing, I wanted to hurl my phone against the side of a building. "Shut up," I muttered.

"You're shittin' me?"

"Go ahead and laugh. Meanwhile, Siren asked me to crawl onto the hospital bed beside her and 'hold her.'"

"And she wasn't playin' you?"

"First thing I thought, but she was dead serious."

Hammer laughed again.

"What do I do?"

"What do you mean?"

"Should I tell her?"

"Tell her what? That she hates the ground you walk on?"

"Yeah."

"I don't know, Smoke. What do the doctors say?"

I told him how hard it had been to get any kind of answer out of the surgeon.

"I'd wait. Maybe in a day or two, her memory will return."

"There's something else."

Hammer was laughing so hard he could barely talk. "Wait. Don't tell me. She's pregnant?"

"You're an asshole."

"Sure am."

"She's also having trouble controlling movement on the left side of her body. If IMI gets wind of this…"

Hammer stopped laughing. "It'll mean the end of her career."

"Glad you're finally taking this seriously."

"Who knows about this?"

"Outside of the hospital staff, me. Now you."

"You're where?"

"Just outside London."

"Does she have a handler?" Hammer asked.

"I'd have to check with Rile on that."

"Can she be moved?"

I shook my head. Not in response to Hammer, just unsure where he was going with that question. "What are you thinking?"

"Look, I know that you and Siren have had your share of issues, but she's a brother-in-arms, man. Just like anyone else, we have each other's backs."

"I agree, but what are you suggesting?"

"Get her the fuck out of the UK as fast as you can."

"And take her where?"

"You've got that spread in North Carolina."

"Tennessee."

"Yeah. Wherever. Take her there."

"And do what with her?"

"Give her time to recover."

"What am I? A doctor?"

"Smoke, you've got more money than Midas. Hire someone. You know, a therapist or somethin'."

"I don't do this kind of shit, Hammer."

"I've known you for a lot of years, my friend, and there's only one thing I can think of to say in response."

I waited, knowing he wouldn't pull any punches.

"Maybe it's time you thought about someone—something—outside the next mission."

"Siren and I…we…"

"Exactly."

"Exactly, what? I didn't say anything."

He let out a deep breath that sounded more like a huff. "She was shot on an Invincibles' op. Let me make some calls to the partners and see who can step up to help her, since it sounds like you won't."

Hammer ended the call.

Rather than sleeping, I walked. I wasn't paying any attention to where I was going. That wasn't the point. What I needed to do was blow off steam.

Hammer was full of shit. I worked. That's what I did. I didn't have time for, or interest in, relationships. Not even friendships. I could count the friends I had on one hand. There were probably lots more who considered themselves my friends, but to me, they were just acquaintances. I sure as hell didn't have time to play nursemaid to Siren.

I looked up and realized I was back where I started, standing in front of my hotel that was next to the hospital. I went inside and was about to take the elevator up to the surgical floor when I saw the doctor who had performed Siren's surgery. He looked like he was leaving.

"Hey, Doc," I said, standing between him and the exit door. "I have a question about Siobhan Gallagher."

He sighed and looked at his watch. "I told you yesterday that we—"

I held up my hand. "I'll save you the trouble of repeating yourself. What happens when she's ready to be discharged? I mean, if she hasn't regained her memory?"

"In those instances, it's usually up to the family. Our experience is that those who go home, if you will, recover far more quickly."

"And if they don't have family?"

He shrugged. "That isn't my area of expertise."

"What happens?" I pressed.

"Their recovery can be…difficult. At best."

"Thanks." I stepped aside and let the man go by. After a few minutes, I walked in the same direction he had, but then stopped and turned around as the words I'd said to myself earlier repeated. *Siren isn't someone I can walk away from.*

It didn't take a genius to figure out why people like me went into my line of work. While some had families, the majority didn't. It was true for Siren and me both. My father had died years ago, and it had been three years since I lost my mother. If I had to guess, I'd say ninety percent of those who worked in intelligence had no family to speak of. What's more, they were loners. I sure as hell was, and so was Siren.

Hammer said he'd contact the Invincibles' partners and see who could step up to the plate to help her, given I wasn't willing. There wasn't anyone she'd feel comfortable with. Including me—once she got her memory back.

I pulled out my phone and sent him a text. Three words, but he'd know what they meant. *I got this.*

It wasn't more than ten seconds before I received his response. *Proud of you, Smoke.*

Siren was awake when I got upstairs.

"You look like hell," she said when I walked in.

I smiled and pulled up a chair. "Any change?"

She rested her head against the pillow, closed her eyes, and then opened them a few seconds later. "No."

"Hey, now," I said when I saw her tears. I scooted the chair closer and put my hand on her arm. "You were shot, kiddo. In the head. Your recovery is going to take a while." I felt her left arm twitch, so I moved my hand. She turned hers over. "See? You're already making progress."

"Because I can turn my wrist?"

I looked up into her blue-gray eyes. "Yes, because you can move your wrist."

"What am I going to do?" she whispered.

I took a deep breath. What I was about to say could change both of our lives, if not forever, for weeks, maybe even months. "Do you remember anything about your family?"

"My mother's dead." Her eyes opened wide. "*I remember.* She is, right?"

"When you were a teenager. Anything else?"

Siren shook her head.

"Your father wasn't a part of your life, and you don't have siblings."

"I'm all alone," she whispered, so softly I could barely hear her even as close as I was.

"You're not." I took another deep breath. "You have me, and this is what we're going to do." I got up from the chair, walked over to the door, and locked it. When I turned around, Siren's eyes were like saucers. "There are things I need to tell you that I don't want anyone to overhear." I sat back down. "Do you remember me telling you that we both work in intelligence?"

"Yes."

"While the mission we were on when you were shot was for a different organization, you actually work for IMI—Irish Military Intelligence."

"Do you work for them as well?"

"I do not. I was with the agency—the CIA—up until a few months ago. Now I freelance. IMI doesn't know the extent of your injuries nor the…challenges you're facing. For your sake, we should do everything we can to keep it that way."

"Why?"

I smiled. "Because you love what you do and you are damn good at it." I never dreamed I'd say those words out loud to Siren, or anything else complimentary.

"I'll lose my job if they find out," she murmured.

"It might be hard for you to get much more than a desk job after this."

"I wouldn't like that?"

"You'd hate it." I laughed and shook my head in disbelief that Siren and I were in the midst of a civil conversation. If her memory suddenly came back, she'd hate the fact that I'd seen her vulnerability even more than a desk job.

"What?"

My phone vibrated, and I took it out of my pocket.

"Do you always do that?" she asked.

"Do what?"

"Answer your mobile in the midst of a conversation."

"Yes," I answered, reading Hammer's text. *Rile will arrange for transport out of London as soon as you're ready.*

"It's very rude, you know."

I looked up at her, then back at my phone. *Copy that. Thanks,* I responded. "Where was I?"

"Being rude."

"Maybe you'll excuse my lack of manners when I tell you that the message I just received was regarding your transport out of England."

"Out of England? Where am I going?"

"To the Great Smoky Mountains in the—"

"Why?"

"Siren—"

"My name is Siobhan, is it not?"

"It is."

"Then, please refer to me by it."

I sat back in my chair, rested my elbow on its arm, and placed my chin in my hand. She may not remember much about her life, but her personality was still intact.

# 4

*Siren*

I hated the way Smoke was smirking at me. On the other hand, he was so *fecking* fine that, if I could, I'd crawl out of this bed and onto his lap.

He was older than me. Maybe by years, given the way his hair was graying and his skin weathered. My guess was the lines edging his eyes were more from frowning than smiling.

Physically, he was huge both in height and breadth, but it was all muscle. His powerful arms, covered in tattoos, strained against the short sleeves of his shirt. His trousers were no different in the way they stretched over the bulk of his thighs.

I closed my eyes and shuddered, remembering the way he'd eased inside me. "More," I could hear myself begging. He'd growled in response, I recalled.

*"Siren?"*

I opened my eyes. "What?"

"Are you listening?"

"Of course I am."

He smirked—again. "What did I just say?"

There was no reason to respond; he knew I had no idea.

He leaned forward and rested his arms on his knees. "What were you thinking about?" he asked in a thick voice.

I looked into his eyes and shook my head.

*"Gnéas?"*

My cheeks flushed, but I raised my chin. "Yes."

Smoke moved the sheet covering me and wrapped his hand around my ankle. He stroked the top of my foot with his thumb. With the opposite hand, he folded the sheet so it rested near the top of my thigh and then moved the hospital gown. I closed my eyes and pushed against the bed, willing his hand to move closer to my slit. As though he could read my mind, his thumb parted my folds and rested on my clit. My eyes shot open when he removed both hands and pulled the sheet back over me.

"Why did you stop?" I groaned.

"Now that I have your attention, I need you to listen to me."

"You're a *feckin' eejit.*"

"Not the worst thing you've called me."

"I'm not surprised."

He squeezed my knee through the bedclothes. "Pay attention, Siren."

I opened my mouth to hurl another insult at him, but shut it. The bastard laughed. "Get on with it, then."

"The team we worked the op for has made arrangements for a private plane to take us from London to the States. Once there, we'll plan for your continued care."

"In hospital?"

"As necessary."

"Why would I agree to this?"

He raised and lowered his eyebrows and then moved the hand resting on my knee up my leg. "Many reasons. We'll make sure you get the medical treatment you need while, at the same time, keeping IMI from knowing the details of your condition."

"Wouldn't they have the means to find out?"

Smoke shook his head. "Not up against the Invincibles. IMI doesn't stand a chance."

"And if I refuse?"

"You won't."

Less than twenty-four hours later, under the cover of night, Smoke carried me out of the hospital, accompanied down a back stairwell by a nurse I hadn't met previously but was told would be traveling with us.

When we arrived at the tarmac of a private airfield, he carried me up the stairs and to the back of the plane, where he gently rested my body on a bed in a stateroom filled with the same equipment as the hospital room.

He watched as the nurse hooked me up to monitors and reconnected the IV.

"This is highly unacceptable," I heard a familiar voice say, but I couldn't place it until I saw the man ushered into the room by two men about the same size as Smoke.

"As I've repeatedly informed you, you'll be generously compensated for your time," Smoke said to the man I recognized as my surgeon.

"I'm not licensed to practice medicine in the States."

"Irrelevant."

"You can't do this."

"I already have." Smoke stepped aside, motioned for the doctor to take a seat, and then leaned down and got in the man's face. "You make sure not a single hair on her head is further hurt, and you'll make more money than you do in a year. You don't protect her life with yours; you won't enjoy the consequences."

"I'll have you arrested for kidnapping."

"Good luck with that." Smoke laughed, as did the two men still standing guard outside the door.

# 5

*Smoke*

"Who are you?" I heard Siren ask the two men who I knew she'd worked ops with previously. I'd forewarned them when they arrived at the hospital of the possibility she wouldn't remember them.

"I'm Jagger," said Mick Reynolds, stepping forward. "This is Vex," he added, pointing to Bronson Dunning. I watched for any sign of recognition, but saw none.

"Nice to meet you," she murmured, looking from them to me. I winked and then motioned the two men out of the stateroom.

"What *does* she remember?" asked Vex.

"Obviously not much about you, since she hasn't thrown anything in your direction," muttered Jagger. "Sorry, man," he added when I shot him a glare.

"Here's the deal. Are you listening?"

Both men nodded.

"I didn't have time to brief you on this before we had to leave the hospital, but Siren believes that she and I are in a…relationship."

Vex opened his mouth and then wisely closed it.

"As far as you're concerned, we're a happy couple. Why, is none of your fucking business."

"Copy that," they each responded, although I didn't miss Jagger's raised brow.

"Right now, your job is to keep an eye on Siren and the doc. That's it."

When they returned to the back of the plane, I reached out to Hammer.

"I was just getting ready to call you," he said.

"What've you got?"

"How far is your place from Asheville?"

"Depends on where." My place, as Hammer put it, consisted of a little over a thousand acres that sat between Gatlinburg and Clingmans Dome on the Tennessee-North Carolina border.

"Biltmore area."

"Two hours tops," I told him.

"There's a fancy new medical complex with a world-renowned stroke-rehab center. Want me to set something up?"

"I'd appreciate it."

"I'll get your final flight leg rerouted too."

"Thanks, Hammer."

"I'd say you're welcome, but I'm doing this for Siren."

"Copy that." I ended the call, knowing he wasn't.

Once in the air, it took nine hours to fly from London to Chicago. From there, it would take another two hours to get to the airport in Asheville. After consulting with the nurse, I agreed to let the doctor fly back directly from Chicago since, so far, all he'd done was tell her to do things she already did without his prompting. I sent Jagger and Vex along with him to ensure he got his money and understood what would happen if he spoke a word about his trip to the States and back.

Every time I checked, Siren was asleep, which was the best thing for her. "You can take a break," I told the nurse, who looked up from the book she was reading. "There are seats in the main cabin or the other stateroom. Whichever you prefer."

She stood, checked the monitors, and walked out, closing the door behind her. I sat in the chair previously occupied by the doctor, whose presence did nothing more than assuage my fear that if something happened to Siren while we were in flight, I would be to blame.

I studied her frail form, wishing I could go back and put myself between her and the bullet I'd been sure killed her.

Had I done so, had it struck me instead, and had I lived, I never would've heard the end of it from her. She would've lambasted me for thinking she needed my protection rather than going after Konstantine von Habsburg.

She didn't remember, and maybe never would, but I had let him go to save her, without knowing if it would be possible, just that I had to try.

"Smoke?" Her eyes opened, and she looked around the stateroom.

"We're in Chicago, still on the plane. The second leg of our flight should be underway soon."

"Where are we going?"

I told her about the stroke-rehab center in Asheville and how I hoped we'd be able to work it out to stay at my ranch.

"Have I been there before?" she asked.

I shook my head. "The mission kept us in Europe for the last few months."

"Tell me about it."

"The ranch or the mission?"

She shrugged. "Both?"

Given I would avoid talking to her about the op during which she was shot, I started with the ranch.

"It sits a mile high on Walter Mountain and has one of the best views there is of the Smoky Mountains."

"What's there?"

"It's a fully operational ranch, so along with the main house, there are other smaller dwellings, barns, and outbuildings."

"What is 'fully operational'?"

"I raise livestock."

"Meaning?"

"Cattle, sheep, goats, horses along with poultry."

"It sounds big."

"About a thousand acres. Oh, and there's a trout pond."

"It sounds like a place I'd never want to leave if I were you."

The older I got, the more I felt that way. These last few months were the longest I'd gone without spending at least a day or two there to get caught up. Home or not, I received regular reports from the ranch manager, but it wasn't the same as riding the property myself.

"I can't wait to see it."

"I can't wait to show it to you." My words were thoughts escaped, and almost startled me. I'd never taken anyone to the ranch, not even Hammer, who had fished for an invitation more times than I could count.

Shortly after we landed at the small regional airport in Asheville, I received a message from Hammer saying he couldn't get Siren an appointment at the stroke center until Monday. It made sense, given today was Saturday.

I carried her from the plane to an SUV that sat, waiting on the tarmac. It would take us to the other side of the airfield where, according to another text from Hammer, a medivac helicopter was waiting.

I had to hand it to him. He had no real idea of the state of Siren's injuries, yet he was one step ahead of me in thinking of things to make travel exponentially easier for her.

One of my ranch hands got out of the vehicle and opened the back passenger door for me. "Hey, Smoke. Welcome home," said Henry "Jack" Gray.

"Thanks. I'll sit back here. You take the front passenger seat," I said to the nurse.

Once inside, I helped Siren lower herself so she could lie with her head on my lap. She looked uncomfortable, but it was the best I could do for the five-minute drive.

Not that she'd ever been a big talker, unless she was bitching at me about something, but Siren's silence unnerved me. "You okay?" I asked, resting my hand on her waist.

"I…uh…thank you for doing this for me, Smoke."

"You're welcome, but what were you going to say instead?"

"Nothing."

We were in flight a few minutes when I looked over to where she lay on yet another gurney and saw Siren studying me.

"I wish I could see whatever it is you're looking at," she said.

"It's nothing but mountains covered by trees."

"I doubt that."

I cocked my head. "Why?"

"Your expression. You look enraptured."

My eyes opened wide when she lifted her left hand and held it out to me. "You have better movement."

"I guess I do." She looked down at her arm as though it wasn't attached to her body.

A funny feeling settled in the middle of my chest. Did that mean her memory would soon improve too? And when it did, would she be angry with me for not telling her the truth about us, that we weren't in a relationship? More that we barely tolerated each other?

"Describe it to me, Smoke."

I turned my head, looking back out at the forests that never failed to take my breath away.

"They say that the Smokies are three million years old. I'm sure there's scientific evidence to back that up, but looking down on them, it's easy to believe. The range is part of both Blue Ridge and the Appalachian Mountains system. The Cherokees were the ones who first called the mountains *Shaconage,* meaning 'place of the blue smoke.'"

She squeezed my hand. "Tell me what you *see.*"

I smiled. "I've never viewed the mountains from this vantage point. The rolling peaks look endless, like a vast, eternal sea shrouded in smoke."

"Why shrouded in smoke?"

"I don't understand the exact science, but over a hundred different species of hardwood trees grow in these mountains. The transpiration of their density, coupled with an average rainfall of eighty-five inches, produces a haze that looks like smoke."

The awe-filled look of wonder on her face as I told her about the place that had been my home most of my life, was unexpected. There was so much I didn't know about this woman. The reminder filled me with a sudden desire to learn everything I could.

Except, until Siren regained her memory, she would likely be unable to answer any questions I asked.

"Were you born here?"

"Near here, in a place called Pigeon Forge."

"Why would that name sound familiar to me?"

I shrugged. "Not too much there when I was growing up. Now it's one of Tennessee's biggest tourist destinations."

She nodded and turned her head away from me.

"Siren?"

"I can't remember where I was born," she whispered. "Where I grew up."

"I can tell you if you'd like."

Her head spun back in my direction. "I would."

"You grew up in southeast Ireland, in a place called Waterford. It's the country's oldest city."

"What else do you know about it?"

I reached over and stroked her cheek with my fingertip. "It's beautiful. Just like the woman who was born there." Her pale cheeks flushed, and she leaned into my hand.

"You've been?"

"My grandmother's family was from Kinsale. It's about two hours from Waterford, so yes, I visited the area."

"But not with me?"

I shook my head. "There hasn't been time."

"How long have we known each other?"

"A few months."

Her next question made the funny feeling settle back in my chest.

"How long have we been in love?"

"Not long," I muttered, having no idea what else to say.

"That's vague."

In that moment of vulnerability, she looked more like a young girl than a woman. The truth was, Siren was a lot younger than me. "Do you remember how old you are?" I asked.

She thought it over for several seconds. "Not precisely."

"You're twenty-six."

"How old are you?"

"I'll be thirty-nine next month." This time, I turned my head away from her.

"Does our age difference bother you?"

"Does it bother you?"

"I hate that," she muttered.

"What?"

"When someone answers a question with a question."

I smiled. "Yes, you do."

"Then, answer."

"I'm too old for you."

"Is it that, or am I too young for you?"

Rather than answer, I leaned over and kissed her cheek.

"The sex, though, is fantastic," she whispered in my ear. "That, I remember."

# 6

*Siren*

My body hurt like *fecking hell,* and my left arm only sporadically did what I wanted it to. My head was wrapped in bandages and, more often than not, throbbed. And yet, given all those things, whenever I closed my eyes, all I could picture was Smoke's naked body covering mine, like it had the night on the beach.

When he went to sit back up and I tightened my grip on his hand, he looked as surprised as I was. "Come closer," I murmured.

He leaned down so I could feel his breath on my cheek.

"Smoke," I whispered. "How much longer until we can be alone?"

A groan emanated from somewhere deep in his chest, and he brought my hand to his lips. "Have you forgotten you were just released from the hospital?"

"Was I? It seemed more like I absconded."

He laughed. A sound I loved. His voice was deep and rich, exactly the way one would think judging by his appearance. Its timbre shot a wave of desire through my body. I moved our clasped hands to my breast and saw the same desire I felt, flare in his eyes.

"Not too much farther," said Smoke, pulling away and sitting up. "I can see the creek that runs alongside the road and starts up at the ranch."

"The creek *starts* there?"

I closed my eyes, picturing what it would look like. An image of a stream flashed in my mind. There were no trees around it, just rolling meadows. When I tried to keep it in focus, it vanished.

"Everything okay?" Smoke asked.

I opened my eyes and looked into his. "A memory…"

"Of?"

"It wasn't much. Just water." Suddenly overcome by sadness, I closed my tear-filled eyes.

"We're here," Smoke said as I felt the helicopter descending. Once it landed, he gathered me in his arms and lifted me from the gurney.

"We're on top of a mountain." I gasped, looking out at the miles and miles of mountain views.

"We're not on the highest peak in the range, but it's close."

I smiled at the pride I heard in Smoke's voice. "What is that?" I asked, motioning with my head at a large structure that sat near the bank of a pond.

"My house."

I was stunned. It looked more like a large mountain lodge.

"Let's get you inside and settled."

"For *feck's* sake, Smoke, you can put me down. I *can* walk."

"We've been traveling for going on eighteen hours. You're more tired than you think."

"It's also time for your pain medicine," the nurse, whose name I couldn't recall but who was walking beside us, said.

"I don't want it," I whispered in Smoke's ear. "I don't need it."

"We'll talk about it once you're in bed."

He carried me up to the front door and waited for the man who'd met us at the airfield, to open it.

"I'll fetch Ms. Wynona, and then the boys and I will start bringing stuff in," Smoke said once we were inside and he set me in a chair.

"Who is that?" I asked.

"She takes care of the place when I'm not here."

"It's about time you showed your face." A very short woman with hair that looked more blue than gray approached. "Welcome to the Blazing T," she said.

"Ms. Wynona, this is the woman I told you about, Siobhan Gallagher."

The woman raised both eyebrows and put her hands on her hips. "You best get Ms. Siobhan into bed, Mr. Smoke. She looks near-dead tired."

"We'll set up in the master," said Smoke, turning to the nurse. "This way."

I shrugged my shoulder when Ms. Wynona winked. "You and I will have plenty of time to get to know each other later," she said as Smoke plucked me out of the chair.

He opened a door and walked into a room that was larger than any place I'd ever lived. "Is this your bedroom?"

"Yes."

"It looks like an apartment."

"Do you want to change your clothes?" he asked, setting me on the bed.

"Into what?" I wore the same hospital gown I'd had on since yesterday and a pair of joggers that were at least two sizes too big.

"We'll see what we can find."

Two other men, who looked just like Jack, brought in medical equipment like what had been on the plane. "Where did all of this come from?" I asked, standing up to stretch my legs.

"I had it delivered." Smoke walked over to me. "Siren, sit back down before you fall."

"Settle yourself, you narky hole. I'm *fine*."

"What did you call me?" He was trying so hard not to smile. I laughed.

"You heard me."

"A narky hole?"

"That's right."

He swept me up in his arms like he had so many times in the last few hours and deposited me back on the bed.

"What is your name?" I asked the nurse, who was busy reconnecting my IV.

"Maureen."

"Nurse Maureen—"

"Just Maureen is fine."

"Okay, well, I do not need any pain medicine at this time. I feel perfectly fine."

"You're lying," she muttered, looking over at Smoke. "And that one threatened me within an inch of my life if I didn't take right good care of you."

"Is it even legal for you to administer that to me?"

She nodded and inserted the liquid from the syringe into the IV port. *"Jaysus fecking Christ,"* I mumbled when the warm feeling coursed through my arm. "I don't want this."

"Excuse us," Smoke said to the nurse, walking up to the bedside with something in his hand. "This should work to sleep in until we can get you some other clothes." He waited until after she left the room before helping me out of the hospital gown and then into the shirt that had to belong to him, based on its size.

"Sweatpants on or off?"

"Off."

He moved the shirt out of his way and tugged the joggers off the lower half of my body.

"You'll need underwear," he said, his gaze focused on my bareness.

"You mean knickers? I never wear them." I looked into his eyes. Two things about that statement surprised me. First, that I remembered I didn't, and second, that Smoke didn't.

He pulled the shirt down and then covered me with the bedclothes. "I'll be right back."

I looked down at the artwork on the shirt Smoke had put on me. It was the letter T, and it looked like it was on fire. Blazing T, that was what Ms. Wynona had said. Smoke. Siren. My eyes drifted closed as I muttered other words to do with fire. Heat. *Sex.*

Where was that man? I wondered, again trying to force my eyes to remain open.

# 7

*Smoke*

When I walked into the bedroom, carrying the tray of food Ms. Wynona had prepared for Siren, I saw she was out cold. I set it on the table by the window and pulled one of the chairs over to the bedside.

Then I leaned forward, resting my elbows on my knees, and studied the woman sleeping in my bed. Her memory was coming back slowly, at least in bits and pieces.

Should I tell her now that what she remembered about us had been a one-time thing? She'd asked me how long we'd been in love. Love? Where had that come from? Siren and I detested one another.

But did we really?

Sure, she infuriated the hell out of me. Many times, I thought about wringing her damn neck. But that night, when our inhibitions were lowered, it had only taken a single touch before our mouths were fused together in a frenzied passion. It was a kiss so good, so hot, so everything, that it could only lead to sex.

I could try to convince myself I didn't remember much about it, but I did.

Unable to resist the temptation now, I peeked under the blanket and sheet at Siren's body. As I hoped, my t-shirt had ridden up, exposing her bare pussy.

I closed my eyes, remembering how she'd tasted that night when I spread her legs and devoured her with my mouth.

She'd said she remembered that sex between us was fantastic, and she was right. I leaned farther forward and kissed the bare skin of her hip and felt her fingers weave into my hair.

*"Smoke, touch me,"* she pleaded, pushing the bed-clothes away and spreading her legs just slightly.

I sat on the edge of the bed and looked into her eyes.

*"Please,"* she mewled.

"Open more for me." I placed both of my hands on the inside of her thighs and used my thumbs to part her folds. I leaned down and ran the tip of my tongue from just above her opening, up to her clit. I pressed hard against it at the same time I eased two fingers into her wet heat.

She writhed as I continued my gentle assault and pulled back when I felt her tighten around my fingers.

"No," she moaned. "Don't stop."

I licked through her folds again, reminding myself to take it slow. Give her pleasure. Nothing more. When her body clenched my fingers again, I didn't stop.

"Come on, let go," I murmured, watching her face as she did as I told her. Her eyes opened and bored into mine.

"Smoke…I…I…"

I moved up her body and kissed her, thrusting my tongue into her mouth. Whatever she was about to say, I couldn't let her.

Tonight, I gave her pleasure, and in the morning, I'd tell her the truth. I had to. Nothing good could come of me continuing to let her believe there was something more between us than there really was.

"Will you stay with me?" Siren asked when I stood and covered her body with the sheet and blanket.

"I think you'll sleep better if I stay in the other room."

"For a little while, then?"

"Sure." I walked around to the other side of the bed and lay on top of the blanket.

When the nurse knocked on the door a little while later, I got up, let her in, and then went to the bedroom across the hallway.

I opened my eyes, surprised it was daylight, and got up to check on Siren. After rapping on the door, I eased it open. The bed was empty, the monitors were turned off, and I didn't see her IV pole.

I walked down the hallway in search of her. Seeing me, Ms. Wynona rushed out of the kitchen. "Shh," she said, putting a finger in front of her lips. "Ms. Gallagher is sleeping."

"Where?"

She pointed over to the sunroom just off the main living area of the house. I could see her IV pole and the nurse sitting in a chair close to the daybed.

When I walked over, she looked up, stood, and led me in the opposite direction.

"Siobhan had a rough night. I've just gotten her back to sleep."

"What happened?"

"I gave her this so she could call me if needed." The woman held up a small device.

"What is that?"

"It's a caregiver's pager, sir."

"You said she had a rough night."

"Yes. I came in, and she was complaining of a terrible headache. I gave her something for the pain and then stayed until after she fell asleep. It wasn't long before she woke again, this time saying she'd had a nightmare. It wasn't until the sun rose that she was able to settle herself enough to sleep."

"Did she say anything about the nightmare?"

"Not specifically, but I do believe she was dreaming about the accident."

"Let me see that thing." I held my hand out, and she placed it in my palm.

"It's just a simple pager, sir."

I gave it back to her without apology. Years of working in the intelligence business had made me suspicious of what sometimes turned out to be the simplest things.

"I'd like to suggest you arrange for Ms. Gallagher to speak to someone, sir."

"Someone as in a psychiatrist?"

The woman nodded.

I walked back into the main part of the house and sent a text to Hammer. *Call when you get this.*

The phone immediately rang. "*Whadaya* need?" he asked.

I told him about Siren's night and what the nurse had suggested.

"Let me make some calls, and I'll see what I can get set up."

"I can do that myself, Hammer."

"Sure you can," were the last words I heard before he ended the call.

I went into my bedroom closet and grabbed a pair of jeans to put on in place of the sweatpants I was wearing. I finished getting dressed and went out to the barn, hoping to find Zeke Jennings, the man who managed the ranch, whether I was home or away.

"Hey, Smoke," he said when I walked into his office. "I heard you were back. I would've come up to the house, but it was late when I got in last night."

"Anything I need to know?"

He leaned back in his chair. "Same shit, different day."

"How bad is it?"

"Best guess is we're down sixteen calves."

While most people assumed cattle rustling was something read about in history books or seen in John

Wayne movies, modern-day cattle thieves cost ranchers like me thousands, even millions of dollars.

Given the Blazing T's location, I'd never thought much about the need for an elaborate security system. The ranch was on top of a mountain, for Christ's sake. "I'll make a call. There's a guy I work with who might be able to help us."

"Ashford?"

"Yeah. You know him?"

"Heard of him."

Asking Zeke how or where he'd heard of Decker Ashford, one of the founding partners of the Invincibles, would likely raise more questions than get me answers, so I let it drop.

"Anyway, I'll contact him and see if I can get something set up."

"Sorry, boss."

"Don't be. With cattle prices skyrocketing and the rest of the economy goin' to shit, it stands to reason that the challenges of our terrain wouldn't thwart thieves forever."

"I hear you brought a woman home with you."

"That's the other thing I came to talk to you about." I told Zeke about Siren being shot, her surgery, and the strokes the doctor said she'd suffered. "I'll be taking her to Asheville this week to meet with a specialist."

"Anything else I need to know?" he asked, repeating almost verbatim what I'd said to him a few minutes earlier.

"She has amnesia."

Zeke's eyes opened wide.

"Siren believes that she and I were in a relationship."

"Were you?"

"Not that it's any of your business, but no, we weren't. In fact, we couldn't stand the sight of each other."

"Interestin'," he said, rubbing his chin.

I got up and walked out of the office. The situation with Siren was bad enough as it was; I didn't need shit from Zeke or anyone else about it.

I was walking along the bank of the creek when I got another call from Hammer.

"*Whadaya* want?" I answered his call like he had mine.

"You're such a bastard. Do you appreciate anything I do for you?"

I laughed. "I thought you were doin' this for Siren."

"You make a good point. Anyway, I've got a guy comin' to the ranch."

"For?"

"Siren."

I held the phone away from my ear and looked at it. Had I never noticed Hammer and Siren worked my last nerve equally?

"Just jokin' with ya. I've got a buddy who lives outside of Asheville. He specializes in PTSD."

"Thanks, Ham. When should I expect him?"

"This afternoon. As a favor to me."

Before ending the call, Hammer gave me the man's name and contact information.

Siren was still asleep when the doctor arrived midafternoon. He introduced himself as Dr. Paul Mansfield and explained that he was a psychiatrist who specialized in post-traumatic stress disorder.

I started to fill him in on Siren's condition, but he held up his hand. "Hammer was able to get her medical records forwarded to me."

How in the hell had he done that? I was the woman's medical power of attorney. "Okay, well, the nurse can fill you in on her nightmares."

After showing him inside, I came back out and sat on the porch, wondering if I should've told the man that Siren believed we were in a relationship that didn't exist.

I'd been sitting in the same place, taking in the views of my ranch for at least thirty minutes when I heard the front door open.

"He'd like to talk to you now," said the nurse.

I walked inside and saw Siren sitting up on the same daybed she'd been sleeping on. The doctor was sitting in the chair the nurse had used earlier.

"How's our patient?" I asked.

Siren looked up at me. "Better," she answered.

"I understand Siobhan will be visiting Asheville to meet with a stroke specialist."

"That's right," I muttered, not knowing whether an appointment had been scheduled yet.

"To make things easier, I'd like to arrange for her and I to meet either before or after the appointment. Whichever is most convenient."

"Whatever you want to do," I said to Siren.

"After," she answered.

The doctor pulled out his phone and tapped the screen. "Let's say Tuesday at three, then."

"I'll walk you out," I said when he stood and said goodbye to Siren. "Do you have a couple of minutes?" I asked, closing the front door behind us.

"Sure."

"Listen, uh, Siren…err…Siobhan—" I stammered.

"You can call her Siren."

"Okay. Well, anyway, with her amnesia, she…uh… thinks that she and I are in a relationship."

"She mentioned you were."

"That's the thing. We weren't."

"I see."

"Maybe I should've told her before now, but—"

He held up his hand. "You were right not to tell her."

"I planned to today."

He shook his head. "Please do not. Right now, you are Siren's rock, if you will. I'm aware she has no family. If you were to tell her that what she believes is her only sense of security is a lie, well, I'm afraid her already tenuous mental and emotional condition may worsen."

"What do I do if her memory comes back? She'll know I've been lying to her."

"It'll be gradual, at best. I'm glad you made me aware of the true nature of your relationship. I'll be there to help her navigate through it when the time comes."

"You said, 'at best.' What does that mean?"

"After reviewing her chart, I'd say there is a chance Siren may never recover her memory entirely."

"Look, Doc—okay if I call you that?"

He nodded.

"When I say that Siren and I weren't in a relationship, what that means is we barely tolerated each other."

"Hammer did share that with me. He also indicated you were willing to care for her until her condition improves."

"That's true, but…"

"But when I said she may never regain her memory, it occurred to you the timeline for her recovery is indeterminate."

"Right."

"I don't know what to tell you, Smoke. Is it okay if I call you that?"

I laughed. "Of course."

"We'll keep the lines of communication open. I'd like to suggest you also schedule time to meet with me. Perhaps while Siren is at some of her other appointments. My assumption is that she'll eventually start physical therapy."

"I don't know if it's necessary for us to meet."

He nodded. "Think it over and know that I can make myself available if you find you'd like to talk."

I watched the doctor drive away. Instead of going inside, I walked over to the barn.

"I'm goin' for a ride," I told Zeke.

"I'll go with you if you don't mind the company."

I motioned with my head for him to follow.

# 8

*Siren*

"Is that Smoke?" I asked Ms. Wynona when she walked into the sunroom.

She looked out the window. "It is. That's Mr. Zeke, riding with him."

"Zeke?"

"He manages the Blazing T."

"Does Smoke have many horses?"

Ms. Wynona sat down in the chair beside the one I'd moved to from the daybed.

"At last count, I believe he had twenty."

My eyes opened wide.

"The Blazing T is an equestrian rescue."

I looked back out the window in time to see Smoke and Zeke ride over the crest and out of view.

"He takes in horses other people don't want?"

"Simply put, yes."

"I sense there's a story there."

She smiled. "I'll tell you if you agree to eat something." She picked up a plate of fruit, cheese, and bread and set it on the table in front of me.

Using my right hand, I picked up a strawberry and brought it to my mouth. "Mmm, this tastes really good."

"We grow them here at the ranch."

"Will wonders never cease," I murmured, picking up a second. "What about the story?"

"Some owners are reluctant to give up their horses."

"What does Smoke do, take them away?"

"Sometimes. If he or Mr. Zeke hear of abuse or neglect."

While I couldn't remember much of anything about Smoke or my own life, it didn't surprise me to hear he'd step in if he thought an animal was in danger. Maybe he did that with people too.

"Mr. Smoke is a good man."

"Yes," I mumbled. "I agree."

"It's that time," said Maureen, approaching with a syringe. After the headache I'd had last night and how long it took to go away, I no longer argued with her about giving me pain medicine.

"You have to stay in front of the pain," she'd explained when it got so bad that she'd gone to the kitchen to fetch an ice pack she then held against my forehead.

"I think I'd like to go lie down in the bedroom for a bit."

"Of course." She helped me wheel the IV pole into the room, reattached and turned on the monitors, and asked if I wanted her to stay.

"I have this," I told her, holding up the pager she'd given me.

"Shall I close these?" she asked, motioning to the blinds.

"Please." I shut my eyes, waiting for her to leave. When I heard the door latch, I opened them and looked up at the ceiling.

I couldn't explain it, but a bad feeling had settled over me when I saw Smoke riding away on the horse. Instead of the intense feelings of love I'd experienced since the first moment I looked into his eyes at the hospital, I felt irritated, even angry with him. He'd done nothing to warrant it.

It took a while, but I finally fell asleep. I don't know how long it was before another nightmare jarred me awake. Instead of being about getting shot, in this one,

Smoke and I were in a terrible row. I opened my eyes, and the man himself was sitting in a chair beside the bed, studying me. I sat up and pulled the bedclothes up to my neck.

"Another nightmare?" he asked.

I nodded, still unable to marry the man in front of me with the person in my dream.

"You're trembling," he said, reaching out to put his hand on my leg. "Do you want to talk about it?"

"Not really."

"Was it the same one you had last night?"

"No."

Smoke stood, walked around the bed, and lay down beside me. "Come here," he said, gently pulling me into his arms. He stroked my cheek with his finger. "It might help you feel better if you talk about it."

"It was about you," I whispered.

"It upset you."

"We were in a terrible row."

His grasp on me tightened, but he didn't say anything.

"Smoke? Did we argue a lot?"

He let out a deep breath. "Sometimes."

"I hated it. I never want to feel that way again."

"Neither do I."

"Promise me it won't be like that between us."

Smoke shifted and put his finger on my chin. "Look at me, Siren."

I stared into his dark brown eyes.

"You and I…we have a lot of passion between us. Can you feel it?"

"I can."

"As intense as it can be when it's good, it's equally so when it's bad."

"What did we fight about?"

He smiled. "Everything."

"Give me an example."

He was quiet for several moments. "We both like to be the boss."

I laughed. "I can see that. What else?"

"We're both very stubborn."

I shook my head. "I'm not stubborn."

He laughed, and so did I.

"If we do have a row, I want us to make up right away." I rested my cheek against his heart. "I hate the idea of being at odds with you."

Smoke kissed the top of my head. "I feel the same."

# 9

*Smoke*

It was only Dr. Mansfield's warning about Siren's emotional state that kept me from confessing everything to her. My throat and chest hurt as I swallowed my deceit deeper with every word I spoke.

Most, if not all, of what I'd said to her was true, but underlying everything was an enormous lie.

As I rode out on the ranch earlier with Zeke, my first instinct had been to put the word out that I was ready for another mission. They'd always come easily to me. Once anyone heard I was available, my phone immediately began ringing.

This time, though, I couldn't run to a place where danger eclipsed the voices in my head that I didn't want to hear. I couldn't escape the things I didn't want to face, by burying myself in the world's problems rather than my own. I had to stick around, be here for Siren, help her heal, and have her back, just like Hammer said I should.

Thinking about Hammer reminded me that I had no idea what he had set up for Siren this week. Mansfield had said he'd see us on Tuesday, but I felt as though she should see someone before that, at least to make sure her incision was healing properly.

When Siren began to softly snore, I thought about easing out from under her, but having her in my arms felt too good. Who knew how long I'd be able to do this without her going back to wanting to claw my eyes out?

I smiled, thinking of the glimpses I'd seen of her old self when she woke up in the hospital outside of London.

If there was something Siren could call me out on, she'd never hesitated to do so. Like when she'd told me she hated it when I answered her question with a question.

Before she was shot in the von Habsburg op, I'd done it on purpose every chance I got, and, man, did it make her mad. I stopped myself from laughing, thinking about the look she'd get on her face, in fear I'd wake her.

I closed my eyes and rested my head against the pillow as I ran my fingers up and down her arm and thought about last night. Desire coursed through my veins from remembering how her hot, wet pussy had clenched my fingers. And the taste of her, God, it was like the sweetest honey. I adjusted my jeans where my cock was straining against the denim fabric.

Siren shifted and put her right arm around my waist. When she slowly moved her hand down to my zipper, I realized the minx was awake.

She squeezed my bulge, and I grabbed her wrist.

"Be careful, little girl," I warned when she tried to twist free of my grasp.

"I know why we fight." She pouted and I released her.

"You seem to forget that you just underwent major surgery."

"You can touch me, but I can't do the same to you? What a load of bullocks."

"When you meet with the doctor, we'll ask. How's that?"

"You want to ask the doctor when we can have sex? *Minus craic*," she muttered, rolling so her back was to me.

"Oh yeah?" I wrapped myself around her and pressed my steel-hard cock against her ass.

"You've made your choice, Smoke. You'll not be getting any from me until you're on your knees, begging for it."

When I was certain Siren had once again fallen to sleep, I eased out of bed and went into the kitchen.

"I'm puttin' the finishing touches on dinner, if you're hungry," said Ms. Wynona.

"Is that country ham and biscuits?" I put my arm around her shoulders when she nodded. "Why don't I spend more time at home?"

"Maybe now you'll have more of a reason to."

I took a step back. "Siren will only be here until she's recovered."

Ms. Wynona pointed to one of the chairs at the kitchen table, and I sat down.

She put a plate of ham and biscuits in front of me. "Your mama raised you with manners, so you eat your dinner with your mouth closed while I tell you what I think."

I smiled and nodded, all too willing to keep my mouth full of her cooking.

"Your soul has been waiting a long time. It was ready when Ms. Gallagher came into your life. Her soul was ready too."

I looked up at her. "It isn't like that."

"I have eyes. I can see what you refuse to. The heart knows when the search is over. Listen to your heart, Mr. Smoke."

"I'm too old for her."

Ms. Wynona smiled and nodded.

I moved my empty plate, leaned forward, and rested my arms on the table. "You want to know the truth? She remembers something that never existed. When her memory comes back, she's going to hate me just as much as she did before. Probably more."

"Did you expect your soulmate would come into your life peacefully?" She laughed and shook her head. "No, child. Ms. Gallagher will make you question everything. She'll make you look at your life with new eyes. She'll make you question yourself, your beliefs. That which you've always been certain of, will no longer be."

"You have that part of it right," I mumbled.

"Oh, but the joy that comes along with it! Not everyone finds it, you know."

I didn't believe I had. Or maybe it was that I didn't believe Siren had. I was certain there was someone else far better suited to her than I could ever be.

I never expected to find someone to spend my life with in the way Ms. Wynona was suggesting. More, I wasn't looking for it, because I hadn't ever wanted it.

I pushed back from the table, grabbed my plate, and put it in the dishwasher. "Thanks for dinner," I muttered, stalking outside.

"I was comin' to look for you," said Zeke, meeting me halfway between the house and barn.

"What for?" I snarled.

"Ashford sent over a proposal."

"Yeah? Since when do you need my help making a decision about something for the ranch? I pay you not to bother me with that kind of crap."

Zeke turned and walked away without saying another word. He didn't look mad, either. That's what I liked about the guy. No bullshit. No nonsense. No flowery fucking words about soulmate shit.

I went to the opposite side of the barn, grabbed a set of keys for one of the ATVs, and took off.

I rode for a solid hour, surveying areas of the Blazing T that I thought might be vulnerable to poachers. There were literally hundreds of access points, none of which were easy terrain to navigate. They had to be coming in and carrying the calves out almost by hand, which also meant they had to be sedating them.

I turned off the ATV and placed a call to Decker.

"Hey, Smoke," he answered. "You get my proposal?"

"I haven't had a chance to review it with Zeke yet. You wanna give me the rundown?"

"It's essentially the same thing we use here at King-Alexander, with a combination of stopgaps and surveillance."

"Got anything that will electrocute them to death?"

Decker laughed. "Not that I'll admit over a cell network."

"As if they aren't secure." I knew they were. Any call made by an Invincibles team member, whether they were a partner like Deck was or a contractor like me, were more secure than what was used by the highest level of the US government.

"Anyway. Look it over, and let me know what questions you have."

"Implementation lead time?"

"About three weeks, only because I can't get there before that."

"Copy that."

"Oh, and, Smoke?"

"Yeah?"

"Rile said to tell you that you owe him an answer."

"I'm solely freelance, Deck. Don't know how many times I have to tell him that."

"He told me to dangle a hefty discount for your security system as incentive."

"What's he got on you, anyway? You were as adamant as I am about staying independent."

"The Invincibles team saved Mila's life. Or helped me do it, anyway."

Mila was Decker's wife, and I'd heard about the op during which she was held hostage by a man who had assaulted her as a teenager. "They would've anyway."

"You're right. But it was the first time it was personal for me, Smoke. There's a different level of gratitude that comes along with it."

I couldn't say I understood, since it had never been for me.

"Like I said, look over the proposal and let me know."

"I don't need to, Deck. Just schedule it, and let me know what you need from me."

"You got it."

I sent Zeke a text, letting him know I gave Deck the go-ahead, started up the ATV, and kept driving.

There was a lot of shit rolling around in my head that I needed to get a handle on. While I understood the reasoning behind Dr. Mansfield's request that I not come clean with Siren, warning alerts reverberated in my chest. There was no question that her reaction after finding out the truth about us would be explosive.

I was about to head up one of the trails that would lead to the main house when something caught my eye. *Tire tracks.* Those fuckers had found a way in, and now that I knew where it was, they'd not make use of it again. I didn't kid myself into thinking that blocking this access would deter them for good, only long enough that we could get Deck's system in place and operational.

I sent Zeke the coordinates of where I was and asked him to bring a crew down here with him. There wasn't much daylight left, and I was determined to get this entry blocked before nightfall.

# 10

*Siren*

It was after ten o'clock, and Smoke still hadn't come back to the house. I was sure of it since I was sitting in the dark, waiting for him.

I wished I could understand the dreams I had about him. In almost every one, he was angry at me. Not just that; I was angry at him too. I couldn't imagine having the heated arguments I saw in my dreams with the man who had been so gentle, so caring, with me since I woke up in the hospital with no memory save for my connection to him.

Given my dreams, I wondered if I was only able to recall part of our relationship. How else could I explain the vivid intensity that flowed from my subconscious? It couldn't be my imagination; I'd never seen the enraged expression on Smoke's face that replayed in my mind. I'd live happily for the rest of my life without seeing him so angry outside of my nightmares.

According to Maureen, in two days, Smoke would take me to Asheville, where I would meet with the stroke specialist, the physical and occupational therapy teams, as well as Dr. Mansfield. The idea of it exhausted me. I was about to get up and go into the bedroom when I heard the front door open.

"Smoke?" I called out when he didn't turn any lights on.

"What are you doing, sitting here in the dark?" Was I imagining it, or did his voice sound like it did in my dreams?

"Waiting for you."

"Siren, it's late. You should be in bed."

"Where were you?"

He walked closer and turned on a small table lamp. "Working."

He looked annoyed and sounded impatient. The muscles in his forearms were taut, and he was filthy.

"What were you doing?"

"It's late," he repeated.

I cocked my head. "That would be the answer if I'd asked the time of day, and a vague one at that."

"I'm not in the mood, Siren." He turned away from me. "Go to bed," he said over his shoulder. When I didn't move, he stalked down the hallway, leaving me sitting alone as I had been for the last few hours.

I got up and switched off the light, picked up the blanket I'd had on my lap, and wheeled my IV pole over to the daybed.

"Everything okay?" I heard Maureen ask from the hallway Smoke had just gone down.

"Fine. I have the pager if I need you."

She walked over to me. "I might as well check your blood pressure since we're both awake."

"Leave it for now," I snapped.

"Very well." She left in the direction from which she came.

I'd been lying on the bed, looking out at the night sky for some time, when I heard footfalls. They were too heavy to be the nurse returning.

"Why are you still out here?" Smoke asked, his tone of voice much softer than it had been earlier. He'd also changed his clothes and looked like he'd showered.

"I don't like sleeping in your bed."

He pulled a chair over and sat beside me. "What's going on, Siren?"

"I have nightmares."

"I'd think you'd have them wherever you slept."

"When I'm in your bed, they're about you."

He leaned forward and rested his elbows on his knees. "Of us, fighting?"

"It's so much worse than that, Smoke." There was enough light from the moon that I could see the pained look on his face. "It's as though you hate me."

"I don't hate you. I've never hated you."

"Was there a time I thought you did?"

His head hung and he shook it. "I didn't say that."

"But you're not shocked by it."

"I told you before that we argued."

"There's something you're not telling me." I rolled so my back was to him, hoping he would leave.

It was a long time before he spoke again. I heard him let out a heavy sigh. "I've lost some cattle, calves mainly, but several thousand dollars' worth. I found one of the places I believe the rustlers used to gain access to the herd. I was out late with the rest of the crew, trying to get it sealed off."

I looked over my shoulder at him.

"I didn't expect you to still be awake."

I wasn't sure what to say, so I didn't speak.

"Come to bed, Siren."

"I'll be fine where I am."

His fingertip trailed down my spine. "I won't be," he whispered. When he held out his hand, I rolled over and took it.

We slept in his bed; neither of us spoke again. When I woke, the sun was up and Smoke was gone. I knew he'd stayed with me, though, since I hadn't had a single nightmare I could remember.

"Come in," I said when I heard a rap on the door.

"Sorry to disturb you, Ms. Gallagher, but are you ready for your breakfast?" asked Ms. Wynona.

"Please call me Siobhan, or Siren if it's easier, and I'll be right out."

"I can bring it in if you'd prefer."

I thanked her but told her I'd rather be up and about.

"Has Smoke eaten?" I asked when I joined her in the kitchen.

"He was up before dawn, Miss…Siren."

"Is he typically?" I asked between spoonfuls of the best steel-cut oatmeal I'd ever had.

"He isn't here at the ranch that often, but yes, he is usually up and gone before I arrive."

"It seems you're always here. I thought perhaps you lived here."

"I do." She pointed out the window at one of the smaller houses. When I turned to look, I saw the can of Irish oats on the counter.

"Do you always have that on hand?" I asked.

"No, no. Mr. Smoke asked me to get it when he told me you'd be staying here."

"That was sweet," I mumbled, shaking my head and wishing I could remember more about him.

"There you are," said Maureen, coming into the kitchen with a syringe and blood-pressure cuff in hand.

I held up my palm. "No pain medication."

To my surprise, she didn't argue. She took my vitals and then sat down to join me for breakfast. Soon, Ms. Wynona had us talking and laughing about growing up in the UK while she told us stories about living in the South.

We were still at it an hour later when Smoke walked into the kitchen. "Sorry to interrupt," he said when the two women with me sprang to their feet. He turned to me. "Do you have a minute?"

"Is everything okay?" I asked as I followed him out of the kitchen.

"I want to talk to you about going to Asheville tomorrow. We'll have to leave early."

"Okay." I waited for him to go on, but he didn't. "Was there something else you wanted to talk to me about?"

"No."

"That couldn't have waited?"

"I just wanted you to know." He stalked out, leaving me wondering what in the world had just happened.

When I returned to the kitchen, both Maureen and Ms. Wynona were gone and all of our dirty dishes were put away.

It was a warm day, so I grabbed a book from the shelf in the main living area and went outside to the front porch. A few minutes later, I saw Smoke stalking away from the barn.

Maybe I dreamed about him being angry because that's the way he was most of the time. But why would I be with someone like that?

"Always a war waging inside that man," murmured Ms. Wynona, startling me.

"Why do you suppose that is?" I asked when she sat in the chair beside me.

"He can't stay still long enough to see the life he desires is right in front of him."

"How do you see that life?"

She reached over and put her hand on mine. "He loves this ranch with all of his heart, yet when he's here, it doesn't feel like home to him."

"Why not?"

"You haven't been here with him until now."

I laughed. "I don't remember much about my life or about our relationship, but the more I'm around him, the more I wonder if we were happy. It doesn't seem like we were."

"You're good for him." She squeezed my hand before getting up to go back inside.

Was I? More importantly, was he good for me?

I didn't see Smoke at dinner and didn't know what time he'd finally come in. I'd asked Maureen to help me move my things to a different bedroom and then, around eight, told her I felt another headache coming on.

The pain medicine she gave me made me drowsy enough that I slept through the night. When I woke, I could see the sun coming up on the horizon.

After unhooking the IV and closing the port the way Maureen had shown me, I took a quick shower and dressed. I didn't have many clothes, and the ones I had, I had no idea where they'd come from.

When I came out of the bedroom, Smoke was standing in the hallway.

"Hello."

"You should pack an overnight bag."

"Okay." I was back in the bedroom and about to ask if he had a bag I could use when he wheeled one in. "That looks like it would hold more than a night's worth."

"You may have to stay longer."

He said "you," not "we." Should I point that out, or would it be best for me to hold my tongue? Given his apparent foul mood, I opted for the latter.

Smoke drove Maureen and me into Asheville and walked us into the medical center for my first appointment.

"I'll check back in later," he said when we reached the door of the doctor's office.

"Wait." I took Smoke's hand and led him away from where Maureen stood. "You're leaving?"

"Did you want me to go in with you?"

"You're joking, right? Smoke, you're the one who insisted I come to America. Now you're just dumping me off with a nurse from the UK who probably isn't licensed here for the kind of care she's been giving me?"

"I thought you'd want privacy."

My mouth was hanging open, and I couldn't find the words to tell him what I thought other than what an absolute *fecking eejit* he was.

"I can stay," he muttered.

"Up and down like a fiddler's elbow," I mumbled.

"What's that?"

"Your moods. One minute you're leaving, the next you're staying. What's it going to be, Smoke?"

"I just said I'll stay."

"You said you can stay."

"I'll stay, all right?"

I stormed back in the direction of the doctor's office with Smoke trailing me. Part of me wanted to tell him to *feck* off. Another part hurt like hell at thinking he could be so cavalier about my medical condition. And finally, the last part wanted to hang onto him for dear life and beg him never to leave me.

# 11

*Smoke*

I listened as the doctor rattled off a slew of acronyms for the tests Siren would have to have. MRI, CAT, PET—I didn't really understand why she needed so many different ones, but what the fuck did I know about medical treatment? I couldn't help but think that someone like Decker should be able to come up with one machine that could do all three things.

Given the uncertainty of how long each would take, the doctor asked if it would be possible for us to stay in the area for at least a couple of days so he'd also have time to review the results.

"Until I know more, I'm going to suggest we hold off on any kind of physical or occupational therapy," he added.

"We're supposed to meet with them next," Siren said to the man.

"They'll need orders from me anyway, so go ahead and meet them. We'll just wait to get your appointments scheduled."

"Will the tests give any indication as to what is causing the amnesia?" I asked.

"That's certainly our hope."

"Will my memory come back?"

"From what you've said, it seems you're suffering from retrograde amnesia as opposed to anterograde—the inability to form new memories."

"That's right."

"Whether your memory comes back and how quickly it might, is dependent upon a large number of factors. I anticipate the damage was mainly in the hippocampus part of your brain, in which case, what we find in the scans should give us a better idea of what to expect."

I watched as Siren processed what the doctor had said. If someone had just told me I may never regain my memory, I don't know if I would be taking it as well as she was. I reached over and took her hand in mine.

"I have a note that you'll be meeting with Dr. Mansfield this afternoon as well."

"Yes," she murmured in response.

He nodded. "Good. Anything else?"

Siren turned to the nurse who was seated in the chair behind us. "Would you excuse us, please?"

"Of course."

"What about physical activity?" Siren asked after the door was closed and we were alone with the doctor.

"I'd prefer to wait until after I've seen your test results to determine what type of physical therapy—"

"I don't mean physical therapy. I mean sex."

I highly doubted that under normal circumstances, a physician would blush at the mention of sex, but he and I both did with Siren's bluntness.

"Ahem. Since you asked a direct question, I'll do my best to answer in the same manner. As I said previously, I will not feel comfortable making a determination regarding physical activity, of any kind, until after I've seen the results of the scans I've ordered."

"Very well, then."

I covered my mouth with my hand to hide the smile I couldn't keep off my face.

"If there's nothing else, stop at the front desk and someone will get the tests scheduled along with your follow-up appointment."

It took several minutes, but eventually, the radiology department was able to schedule Siren for two of the three tests this afternoon and the third tomorrow.

"Do you need to return to the ranch?" Siren asked after we'd left the doctor's office.

That's what I'd planned to do until the ramifications of her never recovering her memory hit me in the head like a steel plank. "I'm not going anywhere."

"If you need to leave, I'll understand. I'm sure you didn't plan to be here more than a few hours."

"Excuse us." Like she had earlier, I took her hand and led her away from her nurse. However, my grasp was much gentler than hers was on mine.

"I'm staying."

Siren turned her head away when her eyes filled with tears. "I feel like an *eejit*."

I cupped her cheek with my palm. "None of this is your fault. You were shot in the line of duty." I took a deep breath and looked up at the ceiling of the corridor. "If you want to know the truth…" I stumbled on my words, trying to mask how emotionally overcome I suddenly was. I leaned down and gently rested my forehead against hers. "I didn't think you were going to make it." I closed my eyes, remembering how panicked I had been in the few seconds it took me to get to her. The immediate sense of loss I felt, unnerved me then and now.

She wrapped her arms around my waist and buried her face in my chest. "I wish I could remember more about you."

And I wished the exact opposite.

While Siren was in with Dr. Mansfield, I made arrangements for us to rent a house within walking distance of the hospital. If Siren had to be here on a regular basis, driving back and forth would wear her out. I also made sure the nurse I'd hired to travel with us was able to stay on.

"I'm happy to stay on as long as I'm needed, Mr. Torcher," said Maureen.

With the amount of money I was paying her, that didn't come as a surprise.

I stepped outside when my cell rang with a call from Rile. "Hello, my friend. I'm sure you know why I'm calling."

It could be one of two reasons, and I said so.

"As much as I want you to commit to becoming an Invincibles' partner, I'm calling for an update on Siren's condition."

"For your knowledge or IMI's?"

"My own."

"We'll know more tomorrow after she's undergone some tests. Any word from Hughes?"

"I was able to burn the details of von Habsburg's escape from the mental facility. As far as Director Hughes is concerned, Siren is still on loan to MI6 until further notice."

"What about Z?"

"He's on board."

Z Alexander was the current chief of MI6 and Rile's former boss. Given the majority of assignments the

Invincibles took on were on behalf of Her Majesty's Secret Intelligence Service, it shouldn't come as a surprise that he would keep the details of Siren's medical condition a secret until told otherwise.

I told Rile I'd be in touch, and was headed back inside when I saw Siren coming out. She looked exhausted and as though she'd been crying.

Instinctively, I opened my arms and embraced her as she walked up to me. "We have an hour before your first scan. Would you like to lie down for a while?"

"I would. I'm so tired."


"What is this?" she asked when I pulled up in front of the furnished rental.

"I thought this would be more comfortable than a hotel."

"You're a very kind man, Smoke."

Siren had called me a lot of things in the time I'd known her. Kind had never been one of them. I wondered if she'd still think so if and when she got her memory back.


"Tomorrow morning, I'll take you shopping," I said when she unpacked the few things she'd brought with her. When she shrugged, I pulled her into my arms. "You're supposed to be resting."

I tugged her over to the bed and lay beside her. When she turned on her side, I pulled her close so her back was against my front. "Try to sleep. I'll wake you up when it's time to go."

"Smoke?"

"Yeah?"

"What if it never comes back?"

I leaned down and kissed her shoulder. "Then, we'll make lots of new memories."

"Do you really mean that?"

"Yes." Probably more than I'd meant anything before in my life.

# 12

*Siren*

When we left the house to return to the hospital, Smoke suggested Maureen take the afternoon off. He was able to stay with me as I waited to be taken in for each of the scans, and just knowing he was there was a comfort.

His words from last night replayed in my mind as I considered what my life would be like if I never remembered anything that had happened prior to being shot. Would making new memories be enough? Would I have a sense of myself without knowing what made me the person I was now?

"Do you feel up to having dinner with me?" Smoke asked when I came out to the waiting area after the second scan was finished. "Scratch that. Let's do takeout instead."

"Do I look that bad?"

"I just realized what a long day you had."

"It's been long for you too."

No sooner were we out of the hospital than Smoke lifted me into his arms.

"What are you doing?" I shrieked.

"Conserving your energy."

"The doctor said we had to wait."

Smoke smiled. "Is everything about sex with you?"

I rested my head on his shoulder. "To be honest, that's all I remember."

Smoke laughed. He didn't chuckle. He laughed. I loved it when he laughed. More, I loved it when I was the one who made him laugh. A memory flashed through my mind so fast I barely caught it, but it was of Smoke. There were a lot of people around us, and even though it was fleeting, I knew I'd said something funny. The thing that confused me was the feeling the memory brought with it. *Surprise.*

"I'm not usually amusing," I murmured.

"What are you talking about?" he asked, setting me on my feet when we arrived at his SUV.

"You don't laugh at things I say often."

He opened the door, and I climbed inside. "It's the life we live, Siren."

When he got in the driver's side, he typed things on his phone while I rested my head against the seat. He was right about my fatigue; all I wanted to do was sleep.

"Where are we?" I asked when Smoke parked on a street where there were several bars and restaurants.

"Picking up our dinner."

"Do you want me to come in with you?"

Smoke shook his head. "I'll be right back."

He was gone mere minutes, and when he opened the back door and set a bag on the seat, the most heavenly aromas wafted from it.

"What is that?"

"Indian."

"It smells fantastic."

"It's your favorite."

The way my mouth was watering over the pungent scents, I knew he must be right, but that I couldn't remember my favorite food depressed me. "What else do I like?"

"There isn't anything you don't like. At least that I know of."

I didn't say much the rest of the way back to the house and then ate very little before telling Smoke and

Maureen that I was retiring to the bedroom. It wasn't five minutes after I crawled under the covers, that I was fast asleep.

When I woke the next morning, Smoke was in bed beside me, his body spooning mine. Instead of bringing me comfort, it troubled me.

What had happened before I was shot that brought these unexpected feelings? Coupled with my dreams about the two of us being angry with each other, I couldn't help but think that maybe we weren't happy together. The idea of it brought me to tears.

I eased out of the bed, used the lavatory, and went into the main living area of the small house. Maureen was in the kitchen.

"Would you like some tea?" she asked.

"I'd love it. Thank you."

"I'm afraid this is all you can have until after your scan."

"I'm not hungry anyway." The anxiety over what I might learn today about my memory left me with no appetite.

One thing the doctor had said during our meeting the day before was that I didn't have to be on the IV any longer, nor was pain medication necessary unless

I felt as though I needed it. That, along with the anti-biotics I'd been given intravenously, I could now take in pill form.

I picked up the steaming cup from the counter with my left hand and then immediately set it back down. My mobility on the left side of my body had improved steadily to the point where I often forgot it wasn't functioning normally. That my hand shook while I held boiling-hot liquid was a quick reminder that I was still suffering from more than memory loss.

"She's not to have anything to eat or drink," said Smoke, coming out of the bedroom, looking both disheveled and sexy as hell.

Maureen pointed to a piece of paper on the kitchen counter. "She is permitted clear liquids."

He nodded and then set about making coffee. Again, the aroma of it brewing stirred something inside me, but I couldn't pull the memory forward enough to know what it was about.

"I like coffee."

Smoke turned to me and smiled. "You do."

"More than tea?" I asked.

"Not that you'd admit."

"May I have some?"

He shook his head. "You like it with cream."

Instead of showering, I took a bath in the tub that was more luxurious looking than the rest of the house. Whoever owned it had left bath salts that smelled of lavender. I sunk into the warm water and closed my eyes. Again, the smell evoked something I could feel but not see.

It seemed as though scents stirred my memory over anything else. Just not enough for me to picture the reminiscence.

I heard a rap at the door. "Come in," I said, putting my arm across my chest to cover my breasts. I moved it when Smoke walked over and sat on the edge of the built-in tub.

"That looks very relaxing."

"There's room for two," I said, winking.

"Maybe two people the size of you, but if I got in, it would overflow."

I reached forward and pulled the plug. "That's easily solved."

"Are you sure?" he asked.

"Hurry before I get cold."

Smoke reached behind him and pulled his shirt over his head and then lowered his joggers to the floor. Seeing his arousal stirred my own.

He settled behind me, and I closed the stopper when the water level was low enough that overflowing was no longer a threat. When I leaned back into him, Smoke put his arms around my waist.

"You have the most beautiful hair," he murmured, kissing the side of my head where the wrapped bandages covered what was now only stubble.

"Do I?"

I felt him nod. "It's inky black with waves that cascade onto your shoulders." He kissed my shoulder. "Your skin is like alabaster, and your eyes…"

"What about my eyes?"

"They can freeze a man's soul."

His lips on my neck distracted me.

"Freeze?" I murmured, leaning into his mouth. "That doesn't sound like a good thing."

"There are times it isn't."

While I wanted to ask more, his tongue running from below my ear down my neck and to my shoulders, left me bereft of thought. When he brought both hands up to cover my breasts, my body writhed of its own accord.

"Touch me," I said, moving one of his hands between my legs.

Smoke cupped my mound, but I wanted so much more. "Please," I begged.

His touch was gentle but nonetheless arousing. His powerful arm kept me still while his fingers pleasured me. Instead of satisfying my craving to feel Smoke inside of me, it made the yearning worse.

"I want more," I whined.

"Soon," he whispered.

"You're playing with me."

"There's no toy I like more."

"Is that all I am? A plaything?" I teased. "Smoke?" I said before he could respond. "Were we happy?"

"It was complicated."

I closed my eyes and took a couple of deep breaths. Did I really need to know? Couldn't I be happy that I was in Smoke's arms and he loved me? Did he love me?

I was about to ask, when I felt his arms tighten around me. "There's no future in our past, Siren."

"But there is a future?"

"I'd like to think so."

"But?"

"I'm a lot older than you are."

"Thirteen years," I murmured, remembering that he'd told me I was twenty-six and he was about to turn thirty-nine.

"That's a big gap."

With so many uncertainties, our age difference was the least of my worries.

This time, Smoke said he'd stay at the hospital with me until they took me in for the scan and then leave once they took me into the room where the test would be conducted. "I'll try to be back before you're finished, but if I'm not, Maureen will wait with you and call me."

I'd ask what he was doing, where he was going, but with despair weighing me down, I didn't really care.

When I was finished and exited into the waiting area, I didn't see Smoke. However, Dr. Mansfield was there, talking to my nurse.

"Hello," I said.

"Siobhan, I was hoping we could take some time to talk." Since Smoke wasn't back anyway, I didn't see why not.

"Sure," I said and then turned to Maureen. "You'll let Smoke know I'll be another hour or so?"

"I will."

I followed the doctor down the corridor and outside to the other building where his office was located.

"I want you to know that Smoke came over and talked to me while you were in radiology. He's concerned about your state of mind."

"Meaning?"

"It would be natural for anyone with retrograde amnesia to be depressed."

I waited until we were inside his office before saying anything else. "I'm remembering things," I began.

"That is very good news."

"Snippets really. Less than that."

"What about that concerns you the most?"

"That what I'm remembering is…troubling."

"Can you give me an example?"

"It doesn't seem that Smoke and I were happy together."

"What is your relationship like now?"

I shook my head and looked out the window. "I don't know what I'd do without him."

"If you had to characterize it in any way, what words would you use?"

"That isn't easy."

"What comes to mind?"

"He cares about me."

"I would agree. Very much so."

"He seems conflicted."

"That doesn't describe your relationship."

"Tentative."

He nodded. "What else?"

"Tenuous."

"Logical that it would be."

The phone on his desk rang, startling me.

"Excuse me. I've been expecting a call from Dr. Taylor."

I cocked my head.

"The specialist you met with yesterday," he said before lifting the phone's receiver. "Arthur. Have you received any results?"

I watched as he listened, murmuring and nodding his head periodically.

"I'm meeting with Ms. Gallagher presently. May I share these results?" He waited a few seconds and then set the receiver back in its cradle. When he walked back over to me, he pulled his chair slightly closer before making notes on the pad he held in his hand.

He cleared his throat. "There is good news I can share with you."

"Go on."

"The MRI and CT scan indicate your brain is healing rapidly. Better than might have been expected."

"But?"

He shook his head. "The other good news is that nothing showed up to suggest there is a medical reason for your amnesia to continue."

"That doesn't sound like good news."

"It is. It means the 'snippets,' as you called them, will likely increase in regularity and, as your brain continues to heal, the details of your memories should become more and more clear."

I wished I felt as happy as the smile on his face suggested he was. Instead, I was filled with a terrible sense of foreboding.

# 13


*Smoke*

I loaded several bags of women's clothing into the back of the SUV and read the text I received from Siren's nurse stating she was currently meeting with Dr. Mansfield.

With each day that passed, I watched Siren become increasingly sullen. While it was to be expected, what I didn't want was for her to sink into a bottomless depression. Whether her memory returned or not, or how quickly it happened if it did, she'd have to find a way to manage her emotions.

Before starting the engine, I called Hammer.

"How's Siren?" he asked.

I filled him in on the tests the doctor had ordered for her. "I called to thank you for making the connection with the psychiatrist."

"I'm glad that's working out."

"She's with him now."

"What about you?"

"I'm headed back there shortly."

"That isn't what I meant. Are you talking to Mansfield too?"

"What do you mean?"

"Come on, Smoke. This wouldn't be easy for anyone to navigate."

"I'm managing."

"Keep me posted." Hammer ended the call, leaving me sitting in the SUV, vacillating between thinking my friend was a pansy-assed pain in my neck or one of the best friends I had. I appreciated that he didn't press me further; if I chose to talk to the psychiatrist, that would be my business.

I drove up in front of the medical complex and saw Siren and Maureen waiting at a table in a courtyard. When I got out, they stood and walked toward me. The look on Siren's face troubled me.

I looked at her nurse, who shook her head.

"Dr. Taylor asked us to come in at one," said Siren.

I looked at my watch. We had a little over two hours. "How about an early lunch?"

"If you're hungry," she responded with zero animation in her voice. It made me want to do something to piss her off just so the fire would come back into her eyes.

Instead, I'd take her somewhere special.

"What is this?" Siren asked when I drove through the gates of Asheville's well-known Biltmore Estate.

"This place was built by George Vanderbilt, Cornelius Vanderbilt's grandson."

"Should those names mean anything to me?" she asked, looking out at the spectacular views of the property.

"Not necessarily. To be honest, I know very little about the family myself."

Siren gasped when we drove through a second set of gates and, to our right, she saw the main house. I stopped the SUV and put it in park.

"It looks like a castle."

"It's the largest privately owned house in the United States," I said, reading over the brochure I'd picked up earlier while shopping. "Would you like to look at this?" I asked, handing it to her.

"Is this where we're having lunch?"

"Not precisely, but we are dining on the estate."

I continued our drive past the vast gardens, along winding roads, until I came to Antler Hill Winery.

"This is lovely," Siren said, stopping to look out at the rolling hills of vineyards. "It reminds me of something."

I walked over and stood behind her. What I was about to do was risky. However, Siren needed to remember things, whether or not that meant she and I would go from lovers back to enemies. Not helping her was selfish on my part. "Close your eyes." I peeked over her shoulder and put my mouth near her ear.

"You and I were in Spain, on the island of Mallorca. We were working an asset-protection op, and one night, there was a meteor shower predicted. We sat on the sand as the full moon illuminated the ocean and the hills of vineyards on the estate."

A tear rolled down her cheek. "I think I remember," she whispered without opening her eyes.

"You looked so beautiful—your pale skin glowed, and the fire I saw in your eyes...I came so close to kissing you."

Her eyes opened. "But you didn't?"

"Not then."

"Why not?"

"A lot of reasons. We were working."

"And yet we were sitting on the beach, looking for shooting stars?"

I turned her in my arms and looked into her icy-blue eyes. "I didn't dare hope you'd want me to."

"I did." Another tear ran down her cheek. "I don't know how I know that, but I do."

I leaned down and kissed her like I'd wanted to do that night. Siren wrapped her arms around my neck, and I slid my tongue between her open lips. I didn't care if the tourists walking to and from their cars saw us or even if it made anyone uncomfortable. I'd stopped myself from tasting her lips that night, and today, I couldn't.

She pulled away first and looked into my eyes. "Thank you," she murmured.

"If you don't mind, I think I'd enjoy shopping a bit before we head back," said Maureen.

"You're not hungry?" asked Siren.

"I'll grab a bite on my own," she said with a wave as she walked away.

"I feel terrible."

"Don't. She looked happy."

"She's probably getting tired of being around me," Siren muttered. "And don't say you are too."

I smiled. "I'd never tire of being with you."

"You're not a very good liar, Smoke."

I led Siren up the steps to the main winery building. Since she couldn't have alcohol until cleared by her doctor and I was driving, we declined the offer of a glass of wine while we sat out on the patio and enjoyed our lunch.

"This was really lovely," she said when we left the estate and returned to the medical complex. The closer we got, the more I could feel Siren's anxiety increase. I reached over and clasped her hand.

"Whatever we learn, we'll face together."

She nodded but didn't say anything.

Rather than go in with us, Maureen offered to remain in the waiting room while Siren and I spoke with the doctor.

"This is healing nicely," he said after he removed Siren's bandages and studied her incision. "We can leave these off."

Siren's hand went to her shaved head, and her eyes filled with tears. I brushed past the doctor and put my hand around her wrist. "It will grow back." I brought her hand to my lips and kissed the back of it. "Let's hear what else he has to say."

She nodded and wiped away her tears.

"As Dr. Mansfield informed you, we see no evidence of a medical reason for your amnesia."

"Might something show up on the other scan?" she asked while I sat, stunned she hadn't mentioned this news during lunch.

"I've received preliminary results, and no, nothing showed up there either."

"Which means?" I asked.

"I believe it is only a matter of time before Miss Gallagher's memory returns."

"That's great news," I said out loud, while inside, I felt like I'd just been given the worst news possible.

"As far as physical activity, I'd like you to begin therapy next week. In the meantime, as long as you don't overdo it, you can resume sexual relations along with light exercise."

"Are there any other restrictions?" she asked.

"Only that you take things slow. Adequate rest will continue to be imperative to your ongoing recovery."

While both Siren and I should be smiling, given the news, neither of us were.

Rather than unloading the things I'd purchased for her earlier in the day, we packed up what we'd taken into the rental house after Siren asked if we could return to the ranch instead of spending another night in Asheville.

She was quiet, sleeping on and off during the drive back while I spent the time wondering if I should disregard Dr. Mansfield's warning not to tell Siren the truth about our relationship.

"I'd like to lie down for a bit," she said once we'd driven through the ranch gates and reached the main house.

"Of course. I'll bring everything in."

When I walked inside and down the hallway, the door to my bedroom stood open. Siren wasn't on my bed, but I saw the door of the bedroom where she'd slept the night before we went to Asheville was closed. I couldn't help but see it as a bad sign.

Siren slept through the night; I knew because I'd checked in on her several times, and when I did, she was softly snoring.

I was more disappointed that she didn't want to sleep in my bed than I was about us not having sex, given the doctor's permission we could. A couple of times, I considered lying down beside her, but if she'd wanted to sleep with me, she would've gone into my bedroom instead of the one she was in.

I left my door open throughout the night and slept only off and on, in case she got up and needed anything. When the sun rose, I got up to check on her again.

"Good morning," I said when I eased the door open and found her sitting up in bed. "How did you sleep?"

"Like the dead," she murmured, her voice hoarse. "I'm sorry."

"What for?"

"I only intended to rest a short while."

"Your body needed more."

She held her hand out, and I sat beside her.

"I feel muddled," she said.

"Understandable." I looked out the window and saw Zeke talking to Jack and one of the other hands. None of them looked happy.

"Do you need to join them?" Siren asked, following my line of sight.

"Not yet."

She pushed against my stomach with her hand. "Go. Find out what's wrong."

The expression on Zeke's face was worrisome enough that I knew she was right. Something was seriously wrong. "I'll be right back."

"Hey, boss," said Jack when I came out the front door.

"Gentlemen, I sense there's something you need to tell me."

Zeke held up his phone without saying a word. What I saw, enraged me. "They just left them for dead?"

He nodded. "Forty down so far. I've got the crew out doing head counts."

Forty head of cattle, slaughtered. Rustling, I understood, even though I hated it. This was something else entirely. This was evil and despicable.

# 14

*Siren*

With every step Smoke took to where the three men stood talking, I could see his body grow increasingly tense. When one man handed him a mobile, even from a distance, I could see how upset he was. Whatever had happened was something horrible.

When he came inside a few minutes later, I was waiting for him.

"I'm sorry, Siren."

"What for?"

"Things have escalated with the rustlers. We've lost several more head of cattle."

"There's no reason to apologize to me."

"Until I can get a new security system installed, the guys and I are going to be out, patrolling twenty-four seven."

"Do what you need to do, Smoke. You have to protect your ranch."

"I may have to have one of the ranch hands take you into Asheville on Monday."

"Let Maureen and I sort that out."

He leaned down and kissed my cheek.

"Let me know what I can do."

He wrapped his arm around my waist and nuzzled my neck. "Know that every minute I'm out there, I'd rather be in here with you."

I felt my cheeks flush but loved his open display of affection. As with everything else, I couldn't remember whether he and I had been in the past. Or even if I was that kind of person. Probably not, given when he'd kissed me so passionately at the winery, I was as flushed as I was now.

When Smoke went back outside, I went into the kitchen. Ms. Wynona was sitting at the table with her head in her hands.

"Are you all right?" I asked.

She looked up, brushed away her tears, and stood. "Yes. Of course. What would you like for breakfast this morning? More oatmeal?"

I walked closer and took her hands in mine. "I want you to sit back down and tell me what's wrong."

"Pay no mind to me, Ms. Gallagher."

"Please call me Siren, err, Siobhan, or whatever you want to call me other than Ms. Gallagher. And I'll warn you, I'll not eat even a speck of food until you tell me why you were crying."

"Did Mr. Smoke tell you what happened with the cattle?"

"Only that things escalated."

"They were slaughtered and left lying on the ground."

I gasped and put my hand in front of my mouth. "How cruel."

She shook her head, pulled a tissue from her sleeve, and wiped her eyes. "Poor, innocent animals."

"Who would do such a thing?"

"Evil people who care only about money."

"But why would they just leave them for dead, then? It doesn't make sense."

Ms. Wynona stood and tossed her tissue in the trash. "I've said too much as it is. He'll be upset with me if I don't make sure you're fed."

"I sense Smoke would never get upset with you about anything, and I can make my own breakfast."

She cupped my cheek with her palm. "Child, sit yourself down and let me do what Mr. Smoke pays me to do."

I didn't see Smoke for the rest of the day, even from a distance. When it grew dark, I went into his bedroom instead of the one I'd been staying in and saw packages sitting on the bed.

"I forgot all about those." I jumped when I heard Smoke's voice from the doorway.

"What are they?"

"For you."

"All of this?"

He nodded, walked over, and stretched out on the bed.

"You need rest. I can do this later."

Smoke fluffed two pillows, put them behind his head, and twirled his finger for me to get on with it. "Start with the purple bag."

I picked it up, set it on the end of the bed, and pulled out several lace brassieres, all in various shades of blue.

"Can you tell what my favorite color is?"

"Pink?" I asked, holding up one of the sheer bras. "I don't think this will cover much."

"That's the idea." Smoke sat up. "Let me see it on you."

"What, now?"

He nodded.

I chose a set and was off to the lavatory.

"Where are you going?"

"To change."

Smoke shook his head. "I want to watch."

"Close your eyes."

Smoke laughed. "Then, I can't watch."

"Just for a minute."

When he did, I quickly removed my clothes along with the less-than-sexy bra I was wearing. I shoved it into the empty purple bag.

"Okay. Open."

Smoke's eyes traveled down the length of my body. Feeling self-conscious again, I brought my hand to my hair.

"Come here," he said, holding out his hand. I picked up the bra and let it dangle from my finger and raised a brow. "Later."

By the time I got to the bed, Smoke had everything off but the joggers he must've changed into before coming into the house. I watched as he shimmied them over his arse and off his body.

"Closer," he said, pulling me so I straddled his waist. He reached up with both hands and palmed my breasts. He toyed with one nipple and massaged the flesh around the other.

"I can feel how much you want me," he said, reaching his hand between my legs, where my wetness dampened the skin of his stomach. He sat up and slowly lowered me so my back was flat on the bed but my legs were still around his waist.

He used his thumbs to spread my folds. "Magnificent," he murmured, caressing my flesh with his fingertip. He brought that finger to his mouth, licked it clean, and then reached over to the nightstand.

He grabbed a foil packet from the drawer and handed it to me. "Go ahead."

I tore it open and rolled the condom down his length. He took my hand and pulled me up. "Wrap your arms around my neck and hold on tight."

He lifted my pelvis up far enough that he could ease into me. "We're going to take this slow, Siren. I want you to watch as I go deeper."

I was mesmerized by the sight of him entering me no more than an inch at a time until my body was flush with his. He put his hands under my bottom and moved my body back and forth. My fingernails dug into his shoulders when he increased the pace and thrust against me. He lay back, bringing me with him so I was in the same position as before, straddling his body, only this time, he was inside me. I slowly moved up and down, my eyes boring into his.

Smoke put his hands on my waist. "Be still," he said, taking over the rhythm of our lovemaking. When I leaned back so I could feel him even deeper, he pulled me forward, grasped the back of my neck, and kissed me. He thrust once more and held my body as close to his as I could be. His mouth ravaged mine as I felt him pulsing inside me while the fingers of his other hand pressed against my clit.

I held my breath as my body pulsated, squeezing every last ounce of pleasure before I collapsed at his side.

"I can only sleep a few hours," I heard him say as I felt myself sinking into a deep slumber. When I woke, it was still dark and I was alone.

A profound sadness settled over me as though, somewhere deep in my soul, I knew that, one day soon, Smoke would be gone from my bed forever.

# 15

*Smoke*

Two weeks ago, I'd called Decker Ashford to see if there was any way we could accelerate the installation of the ranch's security system. He told me he'd see what he could do and get back to me. Today, he'd be arriving with a crew, and by the end of the week, the Blazing T should be close to as secure as King-Alexander Ranch.

Since the morning after we returned from Asheville, Zeke, the rest of the guys, and I worked around the clock, surveilling every part of the ranch. The breaks we took were few and far between, which meant I had very little time to spend with Siren.

Every minute I was away from her, I craved the feeling of her sweet body next to mine. More, I longed to keep my cock buried inside her wet heat as often as I could.

She'd left two days ago for Asheville, and once she finished her PT session today, followed by a session with Mansfield, she and Maureen would be on their way back here.

Siren's nurse had insisted she was perfectly capable of making the drive from the ranch into the city, and when I balked, the woman who could be so sweet and loving when in my arms, turned into the hellcat I hardly remembered. Especially when she lectured me about being a misogynist.

I'd wound my arm around her waist, pulled her close, and told her the next time we had sex, I'd gladly let her be in charge.

"Maureen driving the car and you and I having sex are not the same thing, you *feckin' eejit.*"

Today, I found myself hanging out near the barn, checking the time every few minutes, not in anticipation of Decker's arrival, but of when I'd see my SUV drive through the gates and be able to feel Siren in my arms.

The last two nights, as I lay in bed alone, I reminded myself that my time with the woman who set my blood on fire was temporary. Even if her memory never came back, a woman like Siren would get bored with spending her days in the middle of nowhere on a ranch where there was little she could do.

In terms of her returning to work for Irish Military Intelligence, I would do everything in my power to make sure that never happened. Even if she wasn't with me, I couldn't fathom being able to live, knowing she was putting herself in danger without me being there to protect her.

I heard a vehicle pull in but was soon disappointed to see that while it was a big black SUV like mine, Decker Ashford was sitting in the front passenger seat.

"You're like a puppy waiting for his master to come home and feed him," said Zeke, clapping my shoulder.

"Fuck off," I muttered as I followed him over to where Decker and his team were exiting the truck.

"Smoke," he said, stepping forward to shake my hand. "It's good to see you."

"Likewise, Deck. Thanks for accelerating the schedule for me. I don't know how much longer the guys and I could've kept up the round-the-clock surveillance."

"Copy that," he said. "Okay to set up in there?" he asked Zeke, pointing to the barn.

"All ready for ya," he answered.

My head shot up when I heard another vehicle pulling in.

"That's the rest of my guys," said Decker, maybe catching the look of disappointment on my face.

"He's waiting on Siren," said Zeke once he was far enough away from me that I couldn't throttle him.

"Go do your job, asshole," I growled in his direction.

I walked over to the corral, and Deck followed. "How's she doin'?"

"She's got almost full mobility on the left side of her body, but her memory isn't improving as quickly as her doctors expected it to."

"What's it been, a month?"

"About that."

"Before I put my foot in it, what's the situation between the two of you?"

"We're together." My head snapped up again when I heard another SUV pull in. This time, I saw Maureen behind the wheel. "Excuse me." I raced toward the vehicle, shouting behind me, "Zeke can get you set up."

"Hi," Siren said when I opened the door to help her out.

"How'd it go?"

"Not well," she answered. "I have a terrible head-ache, and I'm not sitting through another one of those *feckin'* scans."

"They did more?"

"Yes," she murmured, walking around me toward the house.

"Siren," I called after her but felt Maureen's hand on my arm.

"She had a rough go of it today."

"In what way?"

"She remembered some things that are troubling her."

"About her and me?"

The nurse nodded. "You might want to let her be for a bit."

That was the last thing I intended to do. I stalked toward the house, down the hallway, past the open door of my bedroom. I opened the door to the other room without knocking. Siren was lying on the bed with her arm covering her eyes.

"Go away, Smoke."

"Maureen said you had a rough day."

"That, I did, and I'm not up for talking about it."

I walked to the window, closed the blinds, and sat on the side of the bed. I moved Siren's arm from her face. "Look at me," I said when she turned her head away. "What did you remember?"

"More of the same."

I hated the anguish I could hear in her voice.

"Why is it in every memory I have, you and I are at odds?" she cried, rolling her body farther from mine and then looking over her shoulder. "I don't want you to answer unless you're going to say something different than what you've said before."

Even if I believed now was the right time to tell her how we'd felt about each other before a bullet almost took her life, with Decker's arrival, I couldn't get into it.

"Get some rest, and we'll talk later."

"Was that Decker I saw you talking to?"

"It was. Why?"

"I remember him."

I left the room and the house with a terrible feeling plaguing me. Could I afford to let this go any longer? If I did, was I risking losing her forever?

Over the next several hours, there was a whirlwind of activity at every part of the ranch as Deck's team and mine began installing the security system that would stop the rustlers from stealing—and killing—any more of our cattle.

When I finally called it a night, one crew was still out riding the ranch, making sure the areas left unmonitored were secure.

Ms. Wynona made sure Decker's crew was comfortably ensconced in the guest houses that usually sat empty save during branding and calving seasons.

All I wanted was to take a hot shower, crawl in bed, and curl my body around Siren's. Heaviness weighed my heart down in the same way fatigue did my body.

When I walked down the hallway, I was surprised to see the door to the master bedroom was closed. I eased it open and breathed a sigh of relief at seeing Siren sound asleep in my bed.

My exhaustion faded away as I went into the bathroom, stripped off my clothes, and let the hot water of the shower melt away the tension I'd carried with me throughout the day. I was rinsing soap from my hair when I felt cold air come from the open shower door.

"May I join you?"

"Am I dreaming?" I asked, running my hands over Siren's naked body. I pulled her against me. "God, you feel good."

"I'm sorry about earlier."

"Don't be." I cupped her cheek with my hand and kissed her.

"I couldn't stand the idea of sleeping alone," she murmured.

"Me either."

I washed her body, and she washed mine. I wrapped her in a towel heated on my warmer, dried myself off, and led her over to my bed. Once under the covers, I pulled her up against me, her back to my front. "I want you more than I want to breathe, Siren, but the old man in me needs to catch a couple of hours of sleep."

I peered over her shoulder and saw she was already out.

At one point during the night, we woke and I took her from behind. At another, I woke and she was straddling me, stroking my erection before sheathing me first in a condom and then in her pussy.

We were four days into the security system installation. Another four, and Decker said everything would be in place—something that would've taken a normal security company a month or more to do. However, there was nothing regular about the system that was now partially functional at the Blazing T.

Zeke and I had spent the morning with Decker while he reviewed what was currently operational and what they still needed to complete.

"Any changes to the original quote?" I asked when he finished the review of the first phase.

"You got an answer for Rile?"

I shook my head.

"Then, it's double." We both laughed.

Zeke stood. "If you fellas don't need me, I'll get back to work."

"We haven't had much of a chance to talk about Siren," said Deck, leaning against one of the desks after Zeke left.

"There hasn't been a lot of change. She's due to head back to Asheville this afternoon. I'm hoping she comes back with more answers."

"If there's anything the rest of the team or I can do, don't hesitate to ask."

I shook my head and looked down at the floor. "Be on standby to sweep up the broken pieces when Siren learns the truth."

"Was it really that bad?"

"You saw us together. The other night, she told me that she had a dream and woke up feeling like we hated each other. She asked me about it."

"What did you say?"

"I told her I never hated her."

"Was that the truth?"

"At this point, I can't say. There were times I sure as hell felt like I did. More times that I almost called Rile and told him that either he partner me with someone else, or I was walking off the mission. Something I had never considered doing at any other time in my career."

"Damn. I didn't realize it was that bad."

"It was worse. There was no question she hated me just as much. More, in fact."

"What I don't get is why Siren thinks the two of you were an item."

"Me either. I mean, there was one night when we were in the Seychelles. We had too much to drink, and one thing led to another."

Decker's eyes opened wide.

"The next morning, I told her that nothing like that could or would ever happen between us again. She was sure to inform me that she'd rather die first. That's how it was between us."

"Damn, Smoke, I'm real sorry."

"Me too. I've wanted to tell her the truth since before we left London. I didn't, and then when we got here, the psychiatrist told me not to. That her already fragile emotional state could get a lot worse."

"What are you going to do?"

"Not much I can, except wait until her memory comes back and, when it does, try to keep her from cutting my balls off and feeding them to me. Then I'm sure she'll go back to IMI and I'll go back to freelancing, only this time, with the caveat that no one ever teams me up with Siren again."

I heard something outside the office, but when I looked, all I saw were the barn cats.

"It seems like you really care for her, Smoke."

"It's more than that, Deck. I think I love her."

"Fuck, man. I don't know what to say."

"Me either. What I said earlier, about sweeping up broken pieces. I was referring to what's left of me."

# 16

*Siren*

Gripping the barn door with one hand, I tightly covered my mouth with the other, praying no sound came out. I ran across the lawn, stumbling before I got to the house. Once inside, I raced down the corridor to Smoke's bedroom.

I pulled out a small bag I'd seen at the back of the closet and tossed some clothes into it, careful to only take what I'd had when I arrived here. Then I went into the bathroom and grabbed a handful of necessities.

Next, I checked the cross-body pouch I wore under my clothes that I'd thankfully found in the bag of things I brought with me from the hospital. In it were my identification, passport, and credit cards.

I hurried over to the bedroom where Maureen had been staying. "Put this inside your suitcase," I said, handing her the smaller bag. "I'll explain later. We'll be leaving earlier than anticipated…um…Dr. Mansfield had to switch my appointment."

"He didn't notify me."

"That's because he notified me," I snapped and turned before stalking out of the room. "Please just do as I ask. I'm begging you."

When she nodded, I hurried back into Smoke's bedroom and packed the suitcase I usually took with me to Asheville. I had it almost wheeled to the front door when I saw him walking in my direction from the barn. I took a deep breath, ready to give the performance of my life.

"I thought you weren't leaving for another hour," he said, looking down at where my suitcase and Maureen's sat near the door.

"I thought we'd get an early start. There are some things I need to pick up at the store."

Smoke wrapped his arm around my waist. "I wish I could go with you."

"Me too. Next time." I leaned forward, brought my lips to his in a quick kiss, and took a step back. "You'd best get back to work," I said, motioning with my head to where Decker was waiting.

"Okay. I'll try to call some time tonight."

"Sounds good. Goodbye, Smoke." I turned away, praying I could get in the SUV without him following.

By the time he loaded the two bags in the back, Maureen was behind the wheel.

"Go," I said before he could walk around to my door.

"Are you going to tell me what's going on?" she asked.

I shook my head, put my finger in front of my lips, and she nodded.

I pressed my fingers against my temples as thoughts raced through my head. There was still so much I didn't remember, but hearing what Smoke had said to Decker gave credence to the dreams I'd had of the two of us, not only at odds, but that left me feeling as though he and I hated each other.

Once we arrived in Asheville, I wheeled my suitcase into the house Smoke had rented. I used the landline to call a car service to take us, along with Maureen's suitcase, to the hospital complex.

"May I use your mobile?" I asked before we left the house. When Maureen handed it over, I walked into the lavatory and rang Dr. Mansfield's emergency number.

"It's urgent I see you as soon as possible," I said when he answered.

"Where are you?" he asked.

"In Asheville, near the hospital."

"I can meet you at my office in twenty minutes."

I ended the call, dismantled Maureen's phone, removed the necessary components, and put it back together. If Smoke had a tracking device on it, from this moment on, it would indicate the phone was here at the rental.

I came out and handed her back the mobile that appeared operational, but wasn't. I heard a car's horn from outside and led her to the waiting vehicle.

Once at the hospital complex, Maureen followed me to an out-of-the-way courtyard and I explained what had happened. My version of it anyway.

"My memory has been coming back in bits and pieces," I explained. "I've no idea what Smoke divulged to you, but he and I work in intelligence."

She nodded, her eyes wide. "I gathered it was something like that, given the way he got the doctor to travel from London to the States with us."

"Right. Anyway, I've received word that I must return to the UK as soon as possible. My orders are that Smoke not know of my departure nor of my whereabouts."

"I understand."

"Do you?" I pressed.

"You can trust me."

Whether I could or not, remained to be seen. I wasn't foolish enough to think she couldn't contact Smoke without her mobile. I only hoped to waylay her if that was her intention. "Best you wait here," I said, before leaving for Dr. Mansfield's office. "I'll be back as quickly as I can."

"I don't have much time," I explained as the doctor closed the door behind me.

"What's happened?"

I told him about the conversation I'd overheard between Smoke and Decker. "The last thing I heard him say was that he was waiting for me to get my memory back. Once that happened, I could return to IMI's employ and he'd ensure the two of us never saw each other again."

The doctor brushed his lower lip with his finger and leaned back in his chair. "I was aware your relationship with Mr. Torcher wasn't the way you remembered it. However, I do believe he cares for you, Siobhan. A great deal, in fact."

"You would think differently if you'd overheard the same conversation I did."

"What are you planning to do?"

"You are not permitted to tell anyone the things we say while in session."

"That is correct."

"My intention is to fly to Washington, DC, and go straight to the Irish Embassy. I will explain who I am and that I need to return to Ireland as soon as possible."

Dr. Mansfield opened a desk drawer and pulled out a large envelope. "This may prove useful," he said, handing it to me.

"What is this?"

"A complete dossier on Siobhan 'Siren' Gallagher."

I opened the envelope, pulled out a few of the pages, and looked through them. "You know everything about *my* life? I don't understand why you didn't tell me."

"Because you needed to remember on your own, Siobhan. Not reconstruct your memory based on things I told you. Do you understand the difference?"

The fact that I did, did not diminish the rage I was feeling at that moment.

"I do not want Smoke to know any of this. That I was here, where I'm going. Nothing."

"There is an easy solution to that."

"What?"

He opened a different desk drawer. "This form removes Mr. Torcher currently from your medical power of attorney. Once you've completed it, he has no legal means by which to access your medical records."

"He could trace my whereabouts that way," I mumbled.

"That is correct."

"Please."

"There's one more thing," Dr. Mansfield said when I stood to leave. "I want you to know that I truly do believe Smoke cares about you, Siobhan. I wouldn't say so otherwise."

"It doesn't matter whether he does or not, because I do not care about him."

"I hope you'll keep in touch," he said as he walked me to the door.

"When I can, I will."

"Best of luck to you, Miss Gallagher."

Before I left his office, I placed a call to another car service and then dismantled my phone. I tucked part of it under the cushion of the sofa in the waiting room. The other part, I dropped in the trash can near the hospital's entrance.

I returned to the courtyard where Maureen sat waiting with her suitcase and asked her to remove the small bag I'd given her earlier.

"Follow me," I said, leading her back out to where the car service I'd called was waiting.

Rather than fly out of the regional airport in Asheville, I asked the driver to take us to the larger one in Charlotte. From there, we'd fly to Dulles in Washington, DC. My plan was to book Maureen and I on a direct flight to London as soon as we landed. However, she'd be the only one of us getting on the plane. Once she did, I would make my own travel arrangements.

# 17



*Smoke*

I'd been trying to reach Siren all afternoon as well as Maureen. Finally, I called Dr. Mansfield.

"I saw her earlier," he told me.

"Did she mention whether she had scans scheduled?"

"She did not."

"Hey, Smoke," Zeke hollered at me. "We've got a situation."

"Thanks, Doc," I said, ending the call. "What's going on?" I asked my ranch manager.

"One of the perimeter lines has been crossed."

This is what we'd been waiting for. That breach would trigger drone coverage; however, I wasn't about to wait around to see if we could identify the bastards stealing and killing my cattle. Zeke, Decker, and I had already formulated a plan of action for when this happened.

"Let's move out!" I shouted, heading for the part of the barn where the ATVs were stored.

*"Fuck,"* I swore into my headset's mic when we came over the crest and could see there was no one anywhere near the breached perimeter.

"We'll review the footage. If someone was here, we'll ID them. If not, I've got a glitch to fix."

"Copy that," I said. "I'm going to keep looking."

"I'll go with you," said Zeke through his own mic.

It was after three in the morning by the time Zeke and I agreed there was nothing more we could do. I'd checked my phone a couple of times, frustrated that I hadn't heard from Siren or Maureen. The latter would be getting an earful from me, given I was the one who paid her salary.

Once back at the house, I showered and got in bed. A few minutes after lying there in utter exhaustion but unable to sleep, I picked up my cell and tracked Siren's. According to the app Decker had developed and put on my phone back when I was hired for my first mission with the Invincibles, Siren's phone was at Mansfield's office since earlier in the day.

Maureen's was at the rental from about an hour prior. While the locations didn't trouble me, the fact neither had updated since that morning, did. Later, I'd have Decker check and see if that app had a glitch too. Knowing the man's reputation, I doubted it very much.

By the end of the second day without hearing a word from either Siren or her nurse, I was equally pissed and worried. Especially after Decker assured me the app was functioning properly.

"Hey, Smoke, I have an update for you," he said a few minutes later.

"Yeah?"

He led me into the office and pointed to something on his laptop.

"What does that mean?" I asked, looking at the flashing alert.

"The phones have been dismantled."

Adrenaline streaked through my body as the ramifications of Decker's words sunk in. I ran my hand through my hair. "What the fuck?" I mumbled under my breath.

"It appears Siren may have more of her memory back than you might've thought."

"What makes you say that?"

"It takes someone with a certain amount of skill to know how to take a cell phone apart in such a way that it still shows up on most normal tracking programs as active."

"You think she's the one who did it?" I asked.

"I do."

"Based on?"

"Instinct."

I nodded. Sometimes, that's all we had to go on. I trusted Deck's gut as much as I trusted my own.

"I'll start searching through security-cam coverage. What do you know about the nurse?"

I pulled up the contact information for the medical personnel placement agency I'd used to find her and forwarded that to Deck.

"While I do this, give them a call and see if they've heard from her."

"Roger, that."

Both he and I realized the time difference simultaneously. "Guess you'll have to wait," he muttered when I calculated it was three in the morning over there.

"We have a hit," he said less than ten minutes later.

"Who?"

"The nurse."

I looked at the screen. "Is that Dulles?"

"Affirmative."

"What time was that?"

"Seven last night."

More than twenty-four hours ago, which meant Siren and her nurse could be just about anywhere in the world by now.

"Is Siren with her?"

Deck shook his head. "She's smart enough to know how to beat facial recognition, Smoke."

In the same way most in the intelligence business would. If one of us appeared on security footage, it was because we wanted to. What surprised me was that Siren hadn't made sure her nurse wasn't recognized either.

"Better read Rile in on this," Deck suggested.

While it was a little later in Spain, it was still the middle of the night, so rather than calling, I sent him a text. *Siren on the move for more than twenty-four hours. Current whereabouts unknown.*

It wasn't five minutes before my cell rang.

"Brief me."

I told him everything Decker and I knew to this point.

"Do you believe her memory has returned?"

"It's the only thing that makes sense."

"I think it's time I contact Director Hughes."

I had to agree. If we were wrong, we'd need IMI's help. If we were right, there was a good chance he'd know her twenty.

"Got her," said Decker.

"Hang on, Rile. Ashford says he has a hit."

"Fuck," I muttered, looking at the image on the screen of Siren walking into IMI's secret headquarters, looking straight at one of the security cameras with her middle finger in the air.

Part 2

# 18



"I refuse to jeopardize our relationship with MI6, the CIA, or the Invincibles by turning this into an international incident, Siren," said my boss, Director Rory Hughes, slamming his fist on his desk. He leaned back in his chair. "It seems to me that Smoke was trying to help you. Not informing IMI of your condition is an issue I'll take up with Rile DeLéon, but you know as well as I do that faced with the same dilemma, both of us would have done the same thing for him or any other agent as he did for you."

I stood and walked over to his office window. I knew he was right; my pride was the only thing refusing to accept it.

"How are you now, Siren?" Hughes asked, his voice taking on a fatherly tone.

To begin, I was humiliated and heartbroken, but Rory wasn't asking about my feelings. He wanted to know my medical condition. A few years ago, before

I'd officially come on board at the Irish Military Intelligence and long before Rory Hughes was named director, he and I had a brief affair. There was no bad blood between us; the flame had just fizzled. When he became my boss, there was nothing untoward about our working relationship. It was as any other I had—except for Smoke and me. It still didn't mean Rory would want to hear the sordid details.

I tossed the copy of my medical records Dr. Mansfield had included in what he gave me before I left his office, but he handed it back to me.

"Tell me how you are, Siobhan."

"The mobility in my left arm is ninety-five percent."

"And your memory?"

That was harder to answer, given on the flight from DC to Dublin, I'd read every word in Mansfield's file. While I'd been furious he hadn't shared my own life with me, now I understood why. I couldn't differentiate between what I actually remembered and the images I conjured based on what I'd read.

I couldn't remember anything about my relationship with Smoke other than what I'd dreamed and then overheard him tell Decker. When I tried to recall anything about him outside of my dreams, it was a blank screen.

"I don't know how to quantify my amnesia."

Rory nodded. "Best to have you thoroughly checked out here in Dublin."

I groaned. That meant more *fecking* scans to sit through.

"Until you're cleared medically, you're on paid administrative leave." He folded his hands on the desk, signaling our conversation was at an end. "Go home and get some rest, Siren."

No one knew it, save Hughes and me, but he was the one who'd given me my code name. It was after he and I'd spent the day out on the water. We were headed back in, and he ran aground on a shallow reef at the same time I happened to be humming.

"You'll lead a sailor to his death, sweet Siren," he'd said that day.

I looked up at him with wide eyes.

"What?"

"A memory."

"Of?"

"That day in Waterford."

"I see," he said, steepling his fingers in front of his mouth. "Do you also remember we weren't together much longer than that?"

"Don't be a *feckin' eejit*," I muttered. "Of course I do. It's just that I remembered how I came to be called Siren."

"A story best kept—"

"You don't need to tell me," I snapped, walking over to his office door.

"I'll expect regular reports."

"When will I be able to return to duty?"

"There is much it will depend upon."

"Understood."

I'd come straight to McKee Barracks from the airport and was anxious to get home, shower, and sleep.

I couldn't help but wonder if Smoke had yet seen the footage of me arriving at IMI headquarters. While the location was secret to most of the world, Smoke had been there, as had Rile. It wouldn't take someone like Decker Ashford long to hack into our security feeds.

That in itself was another memory—or two. I could remember both things in detail. Smoke being in a meeting at the barracks, as well as what I'd read in the dossier on Deck.

My house was a fifteen-minute drive from the office, located in the village of Drumcondra. It was rather big for just one person, with three bedrooms and two baths, but I liked having the extra space. I used one of the bedrooms as a workout room and the other a guest room, even though I almost never had guests.

It also had a converted attic space the agent had suggested I could one day use as a fourth bedroom. Fat chance of me ever needing that. Although it did add to the overall value of the place. The housing estate it was in was very modern looking and quite new, having only been built five years prior.

While it was convenient to public transportation, it would've taken me almost an hour of travel time, so I'd opted for a car service.

When the driver pulled up in front, it occurred to me that I'd also just remembered everything about my house. I shook my head as I unlocked the front door and went inside. I had no idea how long it had been since I was last here, and that had nothing to do with my amnesia. It felt as though it had been months, and it very likely could've been.

I flopped down on the oversized sofa that took up half the living room, too tired to make the trek to my bedroom on the second level.

I closed my eyes and thought about how much warmer than mine Smoke's house had felt the first time I walked inside. It wasn't about temperature. It just felt more like a home. That, of course, reminded me of Ms. Wynona saying he loved the ranch with all his heart, yet when he was there, it didn't feel like home to him.

I couldn't deny my sadness when a tear leaked from my eye and ran down my cheek. I missed Smoke. I hated that I missed him, but I did. But did I miss the *real* Smoke? No. The conversation I'd overheard between Decker and him proved the man who had cared for me, made love to me, was a lie. He was pretending to be someone he wasn't just to…what? Why had he sneaked me away from the hospital in the middle of the night, flown me to the States, and sat with me at the hospital? Was it out of some sort of misplaced sense of responsibility for me?

Or was it that when I woke, I begged him to hold me? I thought about the chaste kiss he gave me when he left that first night. Why hadn't he said something then?

*Jaysus!* I'd made such a fool of myself. Even all alone, I could hardly stand the shame and embarrassment of it.

# 19

*Smoke*

"I've been anticipating hearing from you," said Hughes when I called the next morning. "Either you or Rile."

"Have you seen her?"

"So much for pleasantries, then. Yes, Smoke, I have seen her."

"How is she?"

"I could give you the same perfunctory response Siren gave me. Her left arm has ninety-five percent mobility, and she has no idea how to quantify her amnesia. Or did she say memory? Either way."

It was a struggle not to ask what that meant. Her memory—at least of me—had to have returned, or she wouldn't have staged her dramatic departure.

"Is she…" I couldn't finish. "Thanks, Hughes." I hung up before he could say another word. The man was Siren's boss. Sure, I knew he'd fucked her, but that had been over for years.

When I walked inside the house, Ms. Wynona was waiting for me, wringing a handkerchief.

"Siren is back in Ireland," I told her. I walked down the hallway, went into my bedroom, and closed the door. I knew right away I couldn't stay here. I grabbed a bag, threw some clothes in it, and stalked back to the kitchen.

"I'm leaving."

"I hope you're going to get her," I heard Ms. Wynona say before I slammed the front door behind me.

"Hey, Decker," I said, walking into the barn, where he was messing with something on his computer. "I hate to do this, but—"

"Go do what you gotta do. Zeke, the boys, and I will finish things up here."

"I know you've got to get back to Texas."

"I should be finished tomorrow."

I reached out to shake his hand. "I appreciate everything you've done. Thank you."

"No thanks necessary, but you're welcome. Let me know if there's anything I can do, Smoke."

Since part of Siren's phone had been tracked to Mansfield's office, that's the first place I went when

I got to Asheville. When I walked in, it appeared he'd been expecting me.

"When did her memory come back?"

"I can't answer any of your questions regarding Miss Gallagher."

"Excuse me?"

"You no longer have her medical power of attorney, nor are you listed as someone with whom her medical information may be shared."

Something was way off here. "What's with the sudden formality, Doc?"

"I was able to talk freely with you before because Siobhan permitted it. I can no longer do that."

"She's back in Ireland. The director of Irish Military Intelligence confirmed it."

The man nodded.

"If there's anything you can tell me about her state of mind when you last saw her, I'd appreciate it."

"There's nothing."

I stalked out of his office and slammed the door behind me, just like I had at my own house. The fact that his had some kind of mechanism that *kept* it from slamming, pissed me off even more. "Goddamn son-of-a-bitch," I swore under my breath.

Assuming the stroke doctor couldn't tell me any more than Mansfield had, the next place I went was the house I'd rented.

It was a long shot, but maybe Siren had left something behind, knowing I'd go there.

I tore through the house but didn't find anything other than a suitcase full of the clothes I'd bought her.

What had I expected? That she'd leave a note? "Sorry, Smoke, but I remembered I hate you. Have a fucked life."

I called the nurse placement agency, but they hadn't heard from Maureen. Given I'd paid the nurse directly rather than through them, they couldn't say when they might hear from her again. "She may or may not list with us again," the woman explained.

"If she does, would you please let her know that Broderick Torcher is trying to reach her?"

"Of course."

After that call ended, I rang Decker.

"What can I do for ya, Smoke?"

"Can you continue searching for the nurse? Maureen O'Sullivan."

"You got it."

I walked throughout the house without having any idea what I was looking for, just knowing there had to be something. After an hour, I gave up. Either there wasn't anything, or I couldn't find it.

I drove to the Charlotte airport rather than trying to catch a flight out of Asheville. From there, I flew to Dulles and bought a ticket to Dublin.

I listened as they announced the final boarding call for my flight and then as they announced my name specifically, asking passenger Broderick Torcher to report to the gate for departure.

*What the fuck was I doing?* Was I really going to follow Siren to Ireland? And then what?

There was a litany of truths I knew. First, Siren and I had hated each other from the moment we first met. Second, it didn't matter that my feelings had changed; hers hadn't. Third, even if, by some miracle, hers had too, the bottom line was, I was thirteen years older than Siren. To her, I was an old man. What kind of life could I offer her? One where the two of us would continue following our jobs around the world, each of us in harm's way day in, day out?

The only other option was both of us retiring. I laughed out loud at that idea. No way in hell would Siren give up her job. She was one of the best agents in the business—even at her age—and she had years and years of work ahead of her.

My days were numbered, as much as I didn't want to admit it. I kept my body strong, my mind alert, but no matter how hard I tried, I couldn't stop myself from aging. Getting older was as certain as death.

I tossed the cup of coffee I'd been drinking into the trash and walked out of the airport. I had no idea where I was going, but it sure as hell wasn't to Ireland.

I'd spent two days drunk off my ass, holed up in one of the hotels near the airport. When I woke up the third day, I placed a couple of calls.

By the end of the second one, I was headed out, bag in hand, back to the airport and on my way to California. It had been a long time since I'd worked with Kade "Doc" Butler and his crew.

I needed a break from the Invincibles, mainly because any job I took on for them would be a reminder of Siren and our last mission. As far as I knew, she'd never worked with or for K19 Security Solutions, and I wasn't about to confirm it one way or another.

After flying into the Santa Barbara airport, I met Doc and his wife, Merrigan, at their place in Montecito. As much as I loved my house in the Smokies, I liked Doc's better.

The exterior of the Spanish Colonial Revival house was white stucco with dark brown shutters and a red tile roof, and balconies with wrought-iron railings extended from every upstairs room. Massive palm trees, which looked old enough to have been planted before the house was built, stretched high above the roofline, and bright pink bougainvillea grew up the sidewalls of the five-car garage. The circular driveway was made of Mexican pavers, and large pots full of trailing flowers and vines sat on the edge of the drive and along the walkway.

"Smoke," said Doc, greeting me at the front door. "Welcome. Merrigan will be down shortly."

The inside of Doc's house was no less spectacular than the outside. The main room, just off the foyer, had massive dark wood beams on the ceiling and a fireplace matching the color of the home's exterior at the opposite end of the room.

Dark leather chairs and sofas sat on the tile floors and Mexican rugs. Doc led me into the kitchen, through an informal dining area, and to an outdoor patio bigger than the first floor of the house itself.

Even though it was overcast, I could see the spectacular view of the Pacific Ocean.

"There she is," murmured Doc when Merrigan came outside with two small children. "This is Laird," he said, pointing to a little boy. "And that is Rielle, who is about to turn two."

The little girl looked so much like Siren that it took my breath away. She had dark black hair and pale blue eyes. I couldn't help but wonder if Siren and I were together, if our child would look like Doc and Merrigan's daughter.

After Doc's wife and I cheek kissed, she and their children left us alone to talk.

"What have you got for me?" I asked.

"You know Sumner Copeland, right?"

"Very well." Cope, as he was known, was a handler for the CIA. One of the best in our business. It wasn't long before I left the agency that he'd brought down the then director, a man considered to be the most corrupt in Washington, and who many held personally responsible for the deaths of some of the finest, most professional agents I'd ever worked with.

"He's convinced there were others working with the director, bigger fish."

"There isn't anyone who can get him to talk?"

"According to Cope, his fear of whomever the mystery accomplices are, is greater than a prison sentence." Doc leaned forward. "There's another reason I'm asking you to take this on."

"And that would be?"

"I'm pushing hard for Cope to come on board with K19."

I laughed. "Rile isn't going to like that."

"It's more Decker Ashford I'm worried about."

"Are you aware he just finished installing a security system at my ranch?"

Doc laughed like I had. "It would be a hell of a lot easier if K19 and the Invincibles just joined forces."

I shook my head. "You can't be serious. You know Rile would never let go of that ridiculous name."

"No, you're right. Too many generals, not enough soldiers. What about you, Smoke? Are you still independent?"

"Sure am, and I plan to stay that way."

"Tell me about Siren."

I took a deep breath and looked into Doc's eyes. "Not a subject for discussion."

"Fair enough." Doc told me he'd be right back and went inside. When he came back out, he handed me a folder. "I received this brief from Cope. If you're willing to take this on, I'll put you in direct contact with him, on behalf of K19, of course."

"Copy that," I mumbled. Opening the file, I skimmed the first page. "Fuck," I moaned. "Seriously?"

"You can still decline."

That's exactly what I should do. I should leave the folder on the table and walk out, but I wouldn't. I couldn't. I wasn't in the habit of turning down missions, especially ones that involved the murder of several of my fellow agents.

I took a second look at the three men Cope had named as primary suspects, all of whom were top-ranking officials at Interpol—the International Criminal Police Organization—headquartered in Lyon, France.

The first, Secretary-General Kim Ha-joon, was the former head of South Korea's National Intelligence Service. Second listed was Boris Antonov, Interpol's Vice President, who many believed would eventually be the successor to the current head of United Russia. The last name on the brief was the one that gave me the most pause. Daniel Byrne, the organization's president, was the head of Irish Military Intelligence—Hughes' boss and the man who'd originally recruited Siren.

"Now you understand why I asked about Gallagher."

"Tell me there's nothing in here that suggests she's involved."

"I assure you there isn't."

"Byrne was her mentor."

"Not a mentor, just the man who hired her," said Doc.

"Do you have intelligence to back that up?"

Doc nodded.

"Then, I'm in."

The way Interpol worked, the role of any member of the executive committee, including the president, four vice presidents, and eight delegates, were all unpaid. Each office holder retained their full-time post within their national authority.

Of the three listed in Cope's brief, only Kim Ha-joon from South Korea held a paid position and worked for Interpol full-time.

Two on the outside, one on the inside, all three with close ties to every intelligence organization in the world—some closer than others. Antonov would have a better working relationship with China than Kim would, and so on.

The next morning, I boarded a plane that would take me back from where I came. Cope was currently in DC, but we made arrangements to meet at the CIA headquarters.

"Good to see you, Smoke," he said when I met him on the fifth floor of the building now named for the forty-first President of the United States, George H.W. Bush.

"I thought you retired," I said.

"Thought you did too."

"In the words of that actor in the worst sequel ever made, 'they keep pulling me back in.'"

He led me into a conference room and closed the door behind us. "I guess it's a good sign that I don't have an office here anymore."

After reviewing most of what was in the initial brief and answering the questions I had, Cope and I discussed my cover, which really wasn't much of one. I was headed to France under my own identity, taking on a job for his mole at Interpol—a woman currently working in Secretary-General Kim's office.

# 20

*Siren*

After three days, I was bored out of my *feckin'* mind and I was driving Hughes mad.

"It takes time, Siren," he said. "I understand you were used to being able to see a doctor in the States at a moment's notice, but this is Ireland."

"It shouldn't take a fortnight to see a physician."

"Contrary to what you may believe, IMI has no control over the public health-care system. Find something to do, Siren. Read a book, go for walks in the park. Just leave me alone!"

"He didn't need to hang up on me," I muttered to my mobile.

It wasn't so much my own company I was getting sick of. It was more that I spent every waking moment thinking about Smoke. When I slept, he appeared in my dreams. Twenty-four hours a day with nothing but the Smoke channel playing in my brain, and I had to get out of the house.

I made the trek from Dublin down to Waterford, the place where I was born, just to see if being there stirred any memories of my mother.

I spent the afternoon visiting the cemetery where she was buried and sitting in my car in front of the house I grew up in. I was dismayed when neither brought back a single recollection.

The file Mansfield gave me had something in it about where my mother had spent most of her life working. The shop was located nearby the Waterford Clock Tower that sat on the banks of the River Suir.

After taking a break for a cup of tea, I decided to stay the night. There were several hotels in this part of the city, and given how reasonably priced they were, I went with the swankiest.

While I shouldn't bother, I sent Hughes a text, informing him of my whereabouts. *In Waterford for a few days.*

*Good,* he answered a few seconds later. *While you're there, see if you can find the Irish Crown Jewels.*

I knew Rory was making a joke, but in doing so, I was reminded of the story of their disappearance. I searched it up on my mobile and read the account of the jewels that had gone missing in 1907 and had yet to be recovered.

The star and badge regalia, officially known as the Jewels Belonging to the Most Illustrious Order of Saint Patrick, were last worn by the seventh Earl of Aberdeen on the fifteenth of March at a function to mark Saint Patrick's Day.

After the ceremony, the jewels were given to Sir Arthur Vicars, the Ulster King of Arms, for safekeeping.

It was unclear why Vicars was entrusted with them, but four months later, when the jewels were to be displayed at an Irish International Exhibition in honor of a visit by King Edward VII and Queen Alexandra, the jewels were discovered to be missing.

There were several theories as to who may have stolen them, but no one was more suspect than Vicars.

The stories that surfaced at the time were beyond salacious, including accusing Vicars of hosting drunken—some said homosexual—orgies at Dublin Castle.

One account read: "The police charged with collecting evidence in connection with the disappearance of the Crown Jewels from Dublin Castle in 1907 collected evidence inseparable from it of criminal debauchery and sodomy being committed in the castle by officials, Army officers, and a couple of nondescripts of such position that their conviction and exposure would have led to an upheaval from which the Chief Secretary shrank. To prevent that, he suspended the operation of the Criminal Law, and appointed a whitewashing commission with the result for which it was appointed."

*What in the feckin' hell?* They just gave up the search?

Waterford's connection to the theft, though, came about several years later, in 1920, when James Mallory, a former employee of Arthur Vicars, confessed on his deathbed that Vicars had paid him to transport and hide the jewels in the town's famous clock tower.

An extensive search was conducted, but of course, the jewels weren't found there either.

After spending an inordinate amount of time and money in the Waterford bookstore, I retired to my room, from where I had a picturesque view of the clock tower.

That night, instead of my dreams being filled with images of Smoke, I saw diamonds and emeralds and rubies.

The next morning, I left the hotel in search of James Mallory, the grandson of the man who'd worked for Vicars and claimed the jewels were hidden in the tower. According to the owner of the bookstore, he still lived in Waterford and not far from my hotel.

# 21

*Smoke*

"You damn traitor," said Decker when I answered his call.

I laughed. "You, of all people, should know what it's like being independent. Not to mention, I know all about your history with Doc Butler's family."

"Burns Butler is the best man I know, and I know a lot of 'em." It was well-known through the intelligence community that Doc Butler's father, code name Burns, had mentored Decker in intelligence technology from the time he was a teenager. In fact, many were surprised that when Ashford finally joined a team, he went with the Invincibles over Doc's firm.

"Doc made a joke about why K19 doesn't just merge with you guys, but we both decided that was a train wreck in the making."

"I'll say."

"There must be a reason you called other than to give me shit about taking an assignment from K19."

"It's about Siren."

I took a deep breath. "What you're about to tell me better be fucking good news, Deck. Otherwise, if you've just wasted precious time on small talk, your days on earth are numbered."

The asshole laughed. "I got a hit in Waterford."

That wasn't a surprise, given that's where she was born and raised.

"I did some other checking and don't know what to make of what I found."

"Get to the point, Deck."

"She ran up a pretty big tab at the local bookstore. The subject matter is what I found most intriguing."

"You know what books she bought?"

That shouldn't come as a surprise, given I'd been in France less than twenty-four hours and Deck knew about my current mission.

"Several about the missing Irish Crown Jewels."

"Several?"

"Ten."

I had to admit that was odd. "I thought it was well known that the two pieces were taken apart and sold as individual gems."

"It's one theory."

"All right, you've got me interested. What do you make of it?"

"If I had to guess, she's discovered something that led her to believe she can find them."

I was at a loss as to what to say. Sure, I wanted to know everything about Siren's life, but I wanted to know it firsthand, not from Decker. I wanted her in my arms, in my bed, and in my life—permanently, but that wasn't possible. Even before her memory came back, it hadn't been.

"There's something else you need to know."

"Get on with it, Decker."

"I'm not the only one tracking her."

"Fuck," I muttered. "Who else?"

"Someone at Interpol headquarters. I haven't been able to determine exactly who yet."

I knew from my meeting with Cope that the Interpol Executive Committee was convening this week; it was the primary reason why he was so anxious for me to get started. It would be the only time his three primary suspects would be in the same place at the same time this quarter. My next opportunity to surveil the three men together wouldn't be until October.

"Do you have any idea why someone from Interpol would have their eyes on Siren?"

"Negative, but I sure as hell intend to find out."

"Thanks, Decker."

"I have a couple more updates for you."

"About?"

"Siren's nurse turned up in London. Seems she's taken on another private nursing gig."

I'd wired the remaining funds I owed her before I left the States and headed for France. "Good to know," I said, not really caring other than to know the woman was accounted for. "What was the other update?"

"Your security system at the Blazing T is fully operational. For the time being, I'm receiving the same alerts Zeke gets, and I have mirror monitoring set up. I'll keep an eye on things while you're off playin'."

"You meant while I'm off saving the world. Seriously, thanks, Decker."

"You're welcome. Maybe after this, you'll agree to step away from the dark side."

"Ah, that's gonna hurt ol' Burns' feelings when I tell him what you said about his number one son."

I could hear Decker's laughter as he ended the call.

I didn't like the connection between my mission and Siren one bit. Why would anyone from Interpol be keeping an eye on her? I thought about calling Decker back, but if someone had been watching her while she was at my ranch, he sure as hell would've said so.

The operative Cope had undercover at Interpol was someone who'd worked the same op Siren and I had for Rile. Calla "Casper" Rey had been one hell of an agent, and thankfully, after she walked out of the CIA, the Invincibles team had managed to keep her busy.

I'd known her late husband, Beau Rey, since the early days when we were both green recruits at the Farm. Beau had been killed during a mission in Venezuela, and rumors soon started circulating that the shot that ended his life was from friendly fire. Shortly after the chatter began about the circumstances of his death, the entire mission was burned. No trace of it anywhere.

If I were Casper, I would've done the same thing she did. I probably would've taken it a step further, though, and walked away from the intelligence community entirely.

Like Siren, Casper loved what she did. If she couldn't do the work she'd been trained to do, what might've become of her life? At least by working free-lance, those of us who knew her, and who had known Beau, could keep an eye on her. I was surprised when Cope told me she had taken on the assignment, but he wasn't officially CIA anymore either.

"Secretary-General Kim's office," Casper answered with a perfect French accent. "How may I assist you?"

"Smoke Torcher, reporting for duty, ma'am."

"Oui, Monsieur Torcher, I am happy to confirm your reservation at the Lyon Metropolis, this evening at nineteen hundred hours."

"See ya then."

When we met at the bar later, Casper kept up her French accent when we exchanged hellos, along with her cover name, Angelique Bonet.

"How's Siren?" she whispered after looking around us to see if anyone was close enough to eavesdrop.

"Better." I waited until the bartender, the only person in the room with us, went into the back. "Someone from Interpol has their eyes on her. Do you know who?"

"Byrne ordered it, but it was above my head."

"Do you know why?"

"I listened in on a conversation between Byrne and Hughes. Rory was updating Daniel on Siren's condition and made a joke about sending her off to look for the Irish Crown Jewels while she was on administrative leave."

"What did Byrne say?"

"He asked where she was, specifically, and Hughes told him she was in Waterford."

"Anything else?"

"No, but as soon as he ended the call, he asked me to set up a meeting between him and one of the intel guys."

"Why would he care that Siren was in a turd hunt for jewels that would never be found?" I didn't expect Casper to answer; I was thinking out loud. "Any leads on a connection to  the former CIA director?" I asked.

"Not yet, but there's an off-site meeting scheduled tomorrow between Byrne, Kim, and Antonov."

"No one else?"

"Not that I've been able to find."

"Will you have ears on it?"

She nodded. "And eyes."

"How?"

Casper cocked her head. "How do you think?"

"I thought this was a K19 mission."

"As if Decker could keep his nose out of it."

Under different circumstances, I might've given the man shit about it, but Decker had been in on taking down the director since the very beginning when Cope and another operative grew suspicious about the deaths of some of the CIA's best agents. I couldn't fault him for wanting to see this through to the end.

"What have you got for me to work on while we wait for them to act?"

Casper pulled three files out of her bag. "Three CIA-related cold cases. Make yourself look useful." She looked over her shoulder when the bartender came back in. "Au revoir, Monsieur Torcher."

After Casper left, I went up to my room, opened the first envelope, and reviewed the documents. The case, now ten years old, was known as the La Chapelle-Saint-Maurice killings, named for the town in which the murders occurred. It involved the deaths of three members of a French family, one Brit, and one American citizen. There were two survivors.

While the local French authorities weren't made aware of it, of the five people killed, the Brit was actually an IMI agent, and two others were CIA operatives—the American and one member of the French family, Pierre Martin. Martin's wife and son were also killed in the attack. His two daughters, then aged eight and six, survived with minor injuries.

After five years of investigation, French police said they had "no working theory" to explain the murders and no suspects. Given there was no known link between the three operatives killed, the CIA had no working theory either.

The other two cases Casper gave to me also related to murders of CIA agents that had taken place in France. The first was of a Russian-American double-agent; the second case involved an undercover agent on a mission for South Korea.

There were countless other cases of murdered CIA agents that had gone unsolved, but each of these three could ultimately lead to a connection with Byrne, Kim, and/or Antonov—the very men Cope believed the former director had been working either with or for.

# 22

*Siren*

After more than a *feckin'* week, I still hadn't tracked down James Mallory. I began to think the gobshite was hiding from me.

I'd spent the last several days learning all I could about my dearly departed mother. She was a right saint from the way people talked about her. I began having my own memories of her after the family who lived in the house I grew up in got wind that I was in town and invited me to pop over for a visit.

As I walked through the front gate and up to the door, it was as though I'd traveled back in time. I suddenly felt like a young lass coming home from school.

As I sat in their kitchen, I could see myself having breakfast as my mother fussed about, getting both of us ready for our day. And then doing my homework at the same table while I waited for her to get home from work.

I didn't remember my mother being particularly angelic or mean-spirited. My ma was just my ma.

It was when the woman invited me to look around upstairs that my memories hit the hardest. As I rounded the corner into the room where I somehow knew my mother slept, even without closing my eyes, I could see her lying in the bed where she'd breathed her last breath.

"I'm so sorry," said the woman. "I know your ma was sick for a long time."

"Cancer," I murmured, walking farther down the hallway to the room that had been mine. "Do you have a daughter?" I asked, after opening the door and seeing the same pink-flowered wallpaper that had always been there.

"We did have," the woman said, wiping away her own tears.

"Oh," I said, startled. "My apologies."

"Cancer like your ma. Her name was Siobhan too."

I was overcome by discomfort and wanted to race back down the stairs and out of the house, but the woman had been so kind, I stopped myself.

"Thank you for allowing me a look about."

"You're welcome to come back around anytime."

I nodded, making a beeline for the front door. "Thank you, and goodbye." I was about to close the door when she hollered for me to wait.

"I have something that belongs to you." She came to where I stood in the doorway, carrying a small metal box.

"What's in it?" I asked.

"I've no idea." She pointed to the padlock on the latch. "I couldn't find a key."

"Um, I've walked here from my hotel. Would it be all right if I swung by and picked it up later?"

"Of course. It's been here as long as we've lived here; another few hours won't matter."

I went straight from there back to the cemetery where my mother, along with her parents, whom I'd never met, were buried. I sat down in front of her tombstone, pulled my legs up tight to my body, and wrapped my arms around them.

"Did we ever talk?" I asked out loud, staring at her name etched into the stone. "Why can't I remember us having conversations?"

What no one seemed to know, or was willing to talk about, was who had gotten my mother pregnant. Was it another memory unwilling to reveal itself to me, or had it always been kept from me?

"Who was he, Ma?" I looked up at a man who could be about her age, walking down the sidewalk. He kept going without looking in my direction. "Was it him?" I asked, pointing toward the road. I lowered my head and cried, feeling the pain of missing her for the first time since I set foot in Waterford several days ago.

When I looked up again a few minutes later, I saw an older man rest a bouquet of flowers near a stone a few graves over.

"Sorry to disturb, lass," he said.

"You're not." I got up, brushed off my backside, and walked over to him. "Was she your wife?" I asked.

"Aye. Some sixty years."

I noticed the date of her death was only a little over a year ago. "You must miss her terribly."

"Aye," he repeated, looking down at the etched stone like I had at my mother's. "You're Siobhan," he said.

"I am. Do I know you?"

"It hasn't been that many years, lass."

"You're probably not going to believe this, but I have amnesia."

"You remember your name. That's a good sign."

I laughed. "It is that."

"You and your dear mother lived just down the road from my Janie and me."

"Did we? My apologies, Mr. O'Brien," I said, glancing at the gravestone.

He shook his head. "I've always been Uncle Gene to you."

"Now I feel really terrible."

He smiled and patted my hand when I rested it on his arm. "Don't you dare, my girl."

I pointed toward my mother's grave. "I'll just leave you to your privacy, then."

"On my way home now, anyway. How long are you in town?"

"That's a bit up in the air at the moment."

"I hope to run into you again. Are you staying in the neighborhood?"

"At the Tower Inn."

He raised a brow.

"I know, it's a bit swanky."

"I heard you did well for yourself. Followed in your father's footsteps. He'd be proud."

I felt dizzy and reached out to steady myself. The man caught my arm. "You okay, lass?"

"Did you say, my father?"

"Aye." He led me over to a bench. "You best sit. You look as though you've seen the ghost of my sweet Janie."

"What do you know about my father?"

"I knew him all his life."

I wrapped my arms around my body when I began to shake. Between the memory of my mother dying in her bed and meeting someone who knew not just me but my father too, who I didn't recognize, it was all a bit much. Making it worse was how much I wished Smoke was here with me right now, that having him here would give me comfort.

Mr. O'Brien—Uncle Gene—walked with me back to the Tower Inn. When we stopped out front, he took a deep breath. "Something smells heavenly," he murmured.

I took a deep breath too. "Smells like Irish Stew to me."

"It's been a long time since I've had stew that smelled as good as my Janie's."

"Would you like to join me for dinner?"

"I don't want to be a bother."

"No bother. I'd enjoy the company."

A grin split his face. "Don't have to ask me twice."

Over a pint, Uncle Gene told me that he and "his Janie" never had children of their own, so they "adopted" the kids in the neighborhood. Kids like my mother, father, and me.

"This may sound terrible to you, but I don't remember anything about my father."

He rested his head in his hand, and his eyes hooded. "You wouldn't, lass. You never knew him."

"Why not?" I asked, my voice shaky and thick with the threat of tears.

"He died before you were born."

"H-h-h-ow?"

"I told you earlier you'd followed in his footsteps."

I nodded and brushed a tear from the corner of my eye.

"You've heard of Veronica Guerin?"

"The journalist murdered by John Gilligan's drug gang."

"That's right. Your da was one of the men that tracked Traynor, Gilligan's second-in-command as well as the one said to have ordered Guerin's hit, to Portugal. He died in a gunfight with Traynor."

I sat back in my chair, wondering if I'd known any of this. "What was his name?" I whispered.

"Brendan O'Connor."

"My name is Gallagher."

"Aye. Your mother's name."

"Were they married?"

"They'd planned to be. Everything changed after Guerin's death. Not just in Dublin, in all of Ireland. The entire country became enraged by her killing. Then, after he died, your mother hid the fact you were his child for fear of Gilligan's gang coming after her or you."

"You knew, though."

"Those who knew wouldn't have dared to utter a word."

"It's so sad."

"There were many happy times that came before."

"Yeah?"


Uncle Gene spent the next two hours telling me stories about my mother and father as children and teenagers. "They went from hating each other to loving each other in the snap of a finger," he said, laughing about how all the neighbors had predicted it would happen. "You could tell that, deep down, they carried a torch for one another. That kind of passion burns in both directions. They say it's a fine line between love and hate."

I thought about the conversation I'd overheard between Smoke and Decker. He'd said that there were times he hated me enough to walk out on the mission. He also said I hated him as much, if not more.

Was that why I woke after my surgery believing I'd loved him? Because of that fine line?

"You're lost in thought."

"There's someone…" I shook my head.

"Who you feel the same way about?"

I shrugged. "I told you about the amnesia."

"Go on."

"I don't really know. He and I were on a mission, and I was shot." I pointed to the knit hat I wore whenever I was out in public. "Here," I added, resting my hand on the incision behind my ear. "When I came to in the hospital, I couldn't remember anything. Except him, and by that, I mean I remembered being in love with him and he with me. Turns out that wasn't the case."

"Are you sure?"

I bit my bottom lip. "About me or him?"

Uncle Gene smiled. "You."

"I overheard him say he was just waiting for me to get my memory back. After that happened, he'd make sure we never worked together again."

"Eavesdropping?" he asked with a raised brow.

"Yes."

"Is there a chance, then, that what you heard was taken out of context?"

"I don't think so."

"But you aren't certain."

I sighed and took another sip from the pint that never seemed to empty. "I'm not certain of anything right now, Uncle Gene."

It was late, so rather than let him walk home alone in the dark, I drove him back to my old neighborhood.

"That one is mine," he said, pointing to a house a few doors down from the one I grew up in.

"This might be a long shot, but do you know of a James Mallory?"

"Jimmy Mallory?"

"I suppose so. I've been trying to locate him."

"Here?"

I nodded.

"You've been looking in the wrong place, then. Jimmy Mallory is in Kinsale."

"Did you say Kinsale?" Wasn't that where Smoke had said his mother's family was from?

"Aye. Just so you know, lass, his father was good friends with yours. Best of friends, in fact."

# 23

*Smoke*

I took Casper with me when I went to interview the older of the two girls whose mother and father had been killed in La Chapelle-Saint-Maurice. I was an intimidating motherfucker, and that was by design. It wouldn't serve me well, though, in trying to get a kid to talk about the death of her parents ten years ago.

Casper could be pretty damn intimidating herself when she wanted to be, but she also had a soft side.

"What's the girl's name?" she asked on the ninety-minute drive from Lyon to Lac du Bourget, where the young woman lived.

"Colette. Her younger sister is Emelie."

"Will she be there?"

"I'm not sure."

Casper nodded and looked out the window. "I love this part of France," she murmured. "Beau did too."

"You honeymooned in Paris, right?"

She laughed. "We spent one night there. Beau hated it. I mean, he was impressed by the Eiffel Tower, but otherwise—nope."

I reached over and took her hand in mine. "You doin' okay, kiddo?"

"Better than you are."

"What do you mean?"

"Come on, Smoke, you're miserable. Admit it."

I shrugged my shoulder. "Pretty much always have been, I guess."

"Now you're just full of shit."

"Don't hold back, Casper."

She laughed. "Everyone saw it. There wasn't a person on that op either on Mallorca or in the Seychelles who didn't know that the minute you and Siren stopped arguing, you'd be all over each other."

"She hates me."

"Right."

"The minute her memory came back, she took off. Didn't even say goodbye."

Casper turned in her seat to face me. "Here's the thing, I know the two of you wanted to tear each other's eyes out as much as your clothes off, but Siren isn't like that. I don't see her as the kind of person who would just up and leave."

"Don't know what to tell you since that's exactly what she did."

"Why, though? It seems like there had to be more to it than that."

I had to admit that Siren's abrupt departure stung. And truthfully, now that Casper mentioned it, I didn't see her as someone who did what she did, either. It would've made more sense for her to get in my face about not being honest with her. But to just leave the way she had, maybe there was something I was missing.

"I bet you haven't even tried to contact her."

"Here we are," I said, thankful to end our conversation when I pulled into the parking lot of the restaurant where Colette Martin had agreed to meet us.

Casper and I walked inside and saw only one person in the place.

"Torcher?" asked the heavily made-up woman who had more tattoos than Casper and I combined, plus a greater number of body piercings. She was clad from head to toe in black leather, including her black military-style boots. The only colorful thing I could see on her, other than her ink, was the nail on the little finger of her right hand. It was painted bright orange and was an inch long.

"That's me."

Casper bumped my body with hers when the other woman walked in our direction. "Good thing you brought me along so she wouldn't be intimidated."

While Casper turned her full badassness on, I sat back and listened. Colette remembered some things she said she'd told the police at the time, none of which were in the brief I'd read.

"You said the two other men who were shot that day were friends of your father's?" Casper asked.

"Not just friends, best friends. I told the police that. I followed the reports in the newspapers. They said it was random. It wasn't random."

No one thought the shootings were, probably not even the French police, but that was the standard line when an investigation was taking place and there were no obvious suspects. Let the real killers believe there were no leads, and maybe they'd get sloppy. Only, in this case, it was likely that those carrying out the hit—which is precisely what the CIA, Casper, and I believed it was—were savvy enough to know exactly what the newspaper reports meant.

"Who are you?" Colette asked. "Who do you work for?"

"Interpol," I answered.

She smirked. "Who do you really work for?"

"The same people your father worked for."

She nodded. "Does anyone even care who killed them?"

"Yes," said Casper. "Someone cares very much who killed them."

In the same way there were people who cared about who'd killed Beau. It wasn't just his widow. I cared, and so did every agent who'd ever worked with the man. My gaze met Casper's, and while I didn't speak, I hoped she knew her husband's death was another "cold case" I intended to pursue.

Casper's phone vibrated while we were on our way back to Lyon.

"What's up?" I asked when I looked over and saw her studying it.

"Siren is in Kinsale."

"Kinsale?"

"That's right."

I remembered telling her that was where my mother's family was from. Did she? Even if she did, why would she go there? It certainly wouldn't be to find out more about me. She didn't care enough to do that. Right?

"What are you thinking?" Casper asked after several minutes had passed without me saying anything.

"I'm not sure what to think."

"Do you want my advice?"

"You're going to give it to me no matter what I say, so why ask?"

"Get in touch with her. Jesus, Smoke, go to Kinsale. See her. Talk to her. Do something. Don't just let her walk out of your life for good." With every word, Casper's voice got louder.

"You finished?"

"Nope. You're a fucking asshole if you let Siren go. A fucking, goddamn asshole."

"Nice language for someone who doesn't like swearing."

"I don't like it when other people swear."

I laughed, but then stopped when I saw the look on her face.

"Do you know how hard it is to find love in our line of work? Do you?"

Casper's eyes filled with tears, and she turned her head from me. "Not just in our line of work, Smoke. In life."

"She doesn't love me."

The last thing I expected was for Casper to hit me, but that's what she did. She pulled back and slugged my arm. "Ouch!"

"Like that hurt." She shook her head. "You're such a jerk."

Neither of us spoke again until we were back in Lyon and I pulled up in front of the place where she was renting an apartment.

"Look, Casper, I appreciate everything you said, but I'm here to do a job. I'm not in Europe to track Siren down. If she has anything to say to me, she knows how to reach me. The same can't be said for me knowing how to reach her. Before she left the States, she dismantled her cell phone. In part, so I couldn't track her, but also so I couldn't get in touch with her."

"You keep telling yourself that, Smoke. Give yourself every out you can find, and years from now, when you're sitting in that fancy-as-fuck house of yours on top of a mountain and you're all alone, I want you to think back on this moment and know that it was your choice to be miserable. Some of us have the choice made for us, and some of us are too fucking stubborn and stupid to change things before it's too late." She got out and slammed the car door behind her.

As I told her, I appreciated everything she said, but it wasn't anywhere near as simple as she was making it out to be.

Siren and I were different people than Casper and Beau. We hadn't fallen in love. We hadn't made a decision to spend our lives together. It was the opposite. If the mission she and I were on had ended before she got shot, I would've walked away without a second thought. Siren would've been just another operative I worked a mission with. She wouldn't be someone I dreamed about every fucking night. She wouldn't be someone I missed every fucking minute of the day. Would she?

# 24

*Siren*

I stood in front of the antique shop that looked as though no one had set foot in it in fifty years or more, and double-checked the address. Part of me wished I had it wrong, but I was in the right place. According to Uncle Gene, Jimmy Mallory was in Kinsale, dealing with property he'd inherited when his father, James Mallory Jr., died suddenly a few weeks ago.

According to the records I was able to have pulled when I arrived in town, Junior had inherited it from James Mallory, Sr., the man who, on his deathbed, confessed to hiding the jewels in the Waterford Clock Tower.

I reached out, surprised to find the door unlocked.

"We're closed," someone hollered from the back when a bell affixed to the door rang.

"Jimmy?"

"Who are you?" asked the man, peeking his head around another doorway.

"Siobhan Gallagher."

"Gallagher?" He walked closer to where I was standing, and I could see he was close to my age.

"Gene O'Brien said I could find you here. I understand your father and mine were good friends."

"What do you want?"

"I wanted to ask a few questions about your grandfather."

His shoulders slouched forward, and he rested his hand on a dusty table. "What about him?"

Before I could answer, a sneezing fit came over me. "Sorry," I said when it finally stopped.

"Come in the back. It isn't quite as bad." He motioned with his hand.

"I was sorry to hear your father passed."

"Thanks. Have a seat," he pointed to a chair and then walked over and shut a door. Before he did, I saw an ancient-looking safe in what appeared to be a small storage room. "What do you want to know?"

"I understand your grandfather confessed to transporting the Irish Crown Jewels to the Waterford Clock Tower?"

Jimmy nodded with hooded eyes.

"The authorities searched the tower but found nothing."

"So the story goes."

"Are you suggesting they may have lied?" I asked.

"There are many clock towers in Ireland."

"I'm going to ask you outright, Mr. Mallory. Do you know where the Irish Crown Jewels are?"

"No." While his answer was emphatic, his body language and eye movement were clear indicators he was lying. "Is there anything else?"

"What do you intend to do with the shop?"

He shrugged one shoulder. "I've not decided yet."

"Seems as though there may be many treasures to be found in it."

"Doubtful, even under all the layers of dust."

"You never know. Perhaps you'd even find the lost jewels."

His nervous laugh and the way he blinked his eyes in rapid succession told me I was on the right track. In fact, I'd lay odds that the lost Irish treasure was being held in the safe he hadn't wanted me to see.

# 25

*Smoke*

*Meet me at Lyon Metropolis, urgent,* said the text I received from Casper.

*Here,* I responded.

*Be there in fifteen.*

Shortly after, my cell phone rang with a call from Decker.

"Smoke," he said. "I'm glad I reached you. One of Byrne's underlings is on the move."

"Headed to Kinsale?"

"Yep. Casper already told you?"

"She's on her way here now. My guess is to inform me of the same thing."

"I have a bad feeling."

So did I, and I wasn't about to stay in Lyon while Siren faced danger in my grandmother's hometown, or anywhere else in the world, for that matter.

There was no way around it, I had to fly to Charles de Gaulle first and, from there, to Dublin. Once there, it would take me three hours to drive to Kinsale. Even with the shortest connections, total travel time would be more than ten hours.

According to Casper, the agent Decker had informed me was on the move had a two-hour jump on me. While I waited to board the first plane, I called Deck back.

"Can you get a contact number for Siren?"

"Negative. Already tried."

"Hughes?"

"Won't give it up."

"Why the hell not?"

"Best guess is Siren told him not to."

A growling noise rumbled in my throat. When I got my hands on that woman, and I had every intention of doing so, the first thing I'd do is wring her neck. After that, I'd fuck her senseless.

While I was in flight, both Casper and Decker were gathering as much information as they could regarding Siren's whereabouts now and where she'd been since she arrived in Kinsale.

When I landed in Paris, I had emails from both of them, containing essentially the same information. Five days ago, Siren had visited an antique shop owned by a man by the name of James Mallory, the grandson of a man who'd not only owned the business before passing it on to James' father, but had confessed to hiding the Irish Crown Jewels on behalf of Sir Arthur Vicars, the man last known to be in possession of them.

Her pursuit of solving this mystery was slightly curious although nowhere near as baffling as why the current head of IMI had any interest in her doing so. It wasn't as though the missing jewels had tremendous value. They consisted of only two pieces, valued today at twenty million at best.

They were not even linked to any monarchy but, instead, to the Order of St. Patrick, an elite aristocratic order founded in 1783. The last knight of the order, who would've been the one to wear the regalia, had died in 1974. Even if there had been successors, they wouldn't have owned the jewels; they would merely have been in possession of them.

Apart from it being Ireland's greatest mystery, there seemed to be little reason why anyone would pursue finding them. And then the accolades would only be in notoriety—something Siren wouldn't want or could afford in her line of work.

According to Decker, since her first visit a day prior, it appeared Siren was surveilling the antique shop but, according to the security footage Deck had hacked into, hadn't been back inside.

Once in Dublin, I rented a car and drove to Kinsale. A feeling of foreboding settled in my chest and grew increasingly worse with every kilometer I traveled. Siren was in danger, I swore I could sense it.

I was halfway there when a call came through from Decker. I pulled to the side of the road before answering.

"What's up?"

"I had two agents that were in Dublin take a drive down to Kinsale to visit the antique store Siren's been so fascinated with."

"And?"

"They went in as a couple, and while the woman engaged the shop owner, the man took a look around.

They both reported that the guy, James Mallory, seemed agitated by their presence, particularly when the pair split up. When one of the agents got to the back of the store, he saw an office and, beyond it, an old safe in a storage room. Mallory charged past him and slammed the door closed."

In Siren's words, the *feckin' eejit* just drew more attention to the safe than he otherwise would have. "There's something in it that he doesn't want anyone to know about."

"I'd agree."

"Anything else?"

When Decker said there wasn't, I thanked him and ended the call.

I drove directly to Mallory's antique shop rather than stop again. As I rounded the corner, I was horrified by the sight in front of me.

Fire trucks surrounded what I could only assume was my destination, now a smoldering, blackened shell. I pulled up, parked a safe distance away, and was surveying the scene when I saw someone race past one of the firefighters and into the building—*Siren!*

I rushed past the same men she had. *"Siren!"* I called out. *"Siobhan! Where the fuck are you?"*

I knew she was headed to the back of the shop where Decker said the agents had seen the safe. *"Siren!"* I yelled again, staying low to the ground, hoping to get a glimpse of her through the haze of smoke.

As if it were a special effect, the cloud suddenly cleared, and in front of me stood the woman I'd hated and loved equally in the months I'd known her.

*"Get out of here, Smoke. This is none of your concern,"* she shouted.

"It may not be," I said, taking a step in her direction. "But you are. Let me help you, Siobhan."

"I was never your concern, *Broderick,* except to play with." Her Irish brogue was thick, like when she was about to cry.

"Please." I took another step closer and held out my hand. Before I was near enough for her to take it, I heard a crack above us. I dove in her direction, covering her body with mine as the still-smoldering ceiling came crashing down on us both. Through my thin shirt, I could feel the heat singe my skin and gritted my teeth against the excruciating pain. With one arm, I shoved the rafters off of us and then heard another crack.

"We have to get the fuck out of here."

When Siren didn't respond, I realized her eyes were closed. She was breathing, but the force of my body hitting hers to the ground must have knocked her out. I gathered her into my arms, stood, and raced toward the closest light I could see coming from the back of the building. I was just about to the door when I almost tripped. I looked down and saw a body lying in a heap on the floor.

*"Help!"* I shouted, running out of the building and around to the front. *"There's someone else in there,"* I yelled to men rushing toward me. *"Not far from the back door."*

*"Get a medic!"* one of them shouted in the direction of the truck. *"He's injured!"*

I was within a few feet of what looked like an ambulance when Siren came to and immediately began struggling. *"Smoke, put me down, I have to get back in there!"* she cried.

"Forget the fucking safe; it doesn't matter, Siobhan." I'd set her on her feet, but kept my grip tight on her arm when the pain in my back got so bad I feared I'd lose consciousness.

*"Not the safe, it's Jimmy. He's in there!"* She wrenched her arm away, and we both turned when we heard shouting coming from the building as one of the firefighters ran out with a body in his arms.

*"He's alive!"* I heard one of them shout as they ran past us.

*"Smoke! You're burned!"* Siren screeched, pulling me toward the ambulance. *"We need help over here!"*

I took a step, and everything went black.

# 26



*"Help!"* I screamed when I saw Smoke about to go down, knowing there was no way I was strong enough to catch him. Two guys raced over.

"Get a gurney over here!" one of them yelled, keeping Smoke from rolling onto his back.

I knelt beside him, and he opened his eyes. "You *eejit*, what were you thinking?" I said, cupping his cheek with my palm.

"Had to…save…you." He groaned through gritted teeth as the men shifted his body onto the gurney. I had to turn my head away when I saw the extent of the burns on his back.

"I want to go with him," I said when they put him in the back of the ambulance.

"Not a good idea," said one of them.

"She can ride up front," said another who took my hand and led me to the passenger door.

I prayed the entire way to the emergency room and prayed more when they wheeled Smoke inside.

"Do you know if Jimmy is okay?" I asked the man who'd been driving the ambulance and who was walking me inside the hospital.

"I don't," he answered.

"Are they bringing him here?"

"I don't know." He led me over to a desk. "They'll need some information from you," he said before walking away.

"Do you know the man who was just brought in?" the woman sitting at the desk asked.

"I do."

"Name?"

"His or mine?"

"Both."

In the midst of answering her questions, it dawned on me that I remembered—everything. *I remembered everything.* Every memory I hadn't been able to pull to the front of my brain, was suddenly back.

"Age?" she asked.

"Thirty-eight. He'll be thirty-nine at the end of this month."

"What about family?"

"He doesn't have any." I pulled my phone from my pocket only to find it had been crushed, probably when Smoke landed on top of me.

"Do you know if he was conscious when they brought him in?"

"He was. Um, is there a phone somewhere I could use?"

"Let me get through these questions, and then I'll see what I can do."

A man dressed in scrubs approached from behind the woman. "Are you Siren?"

"I am."

"He's asking for you."

"Are we finished?" I asked, standing to follow when the man motioned for me to.

"I know where to find you if I have more questions."

"I'm Leo, one of Mr. Torcher's nurses," the man who led me into the room where Smoke lay on his stomach with his eyes closed said. "They gave him something for the pain. I think it knocked him out cold."

"Nothing knocks me out cold," Smoke muttered, opening one eye.

I pulled a chair up beside him. "Seems our positions have reversed. Thanks for saving my life, Smoke. For the second time, it seems."

"I'd appreciate it if you'd stop putting yourself in danger, so I didn't have to."

"What are you doing in Ireland?"

"Looking for you."

"Why?"

"You left without saying goodbye."

"I didn't think you'd care."

The door opened, and two other people walked in. "I'm Dr. O'Keefe, and this is Dr. Flynn. We're from the burn unit." The man who'd just introduced himself turned to me. "Young lady, we'll need you to step outside."

I stood, leaned down, and kissed Smoke's cheek. "I'm not going far." Once the door closed behind me, I leaned up against the wall and put my head in my hands. I still had adrenaline coursing through my body, and when it wore off, I knew the crash was going to be a hard one.

"Miss?"

I looked up to see the nurse from the check-in desk. "More questions?"

"No," she said, handing me a phone. "I forgot you asked to use one."

"Thanks."

I rang one of the few numbers I knew by heart.

"Hughes," I said when he picked up.

"Siren. What can I do for you?"

"I need to get in touch with Decker Ashford, and, um, I don't have my mobile."

"What happened to it?"

"It was crushed when I was trapped inside a burning building."

"What did you say?"

"You heard me, Rory. Got Deck's number?"

"Where are you?"

"I've no idea. Hang on." I put one hand over the phone's mic. "Excuse me," I said to someone walking past dressed in scrubs. "What is the name of this hospital?"

"Kinsale Community."

"I heard," said Hughes when I brought the phone back to my ear. "I'm on my way."

"Wait. What about Decker?"

"He's about to call you."

I heard the chimes of the call ending at the same time another call came in.

"Siren, what's happened?"

I told him about my running into the antique shop to look for the man I knew was still inside, Smoke coming in after me, and that he'd been burned when smoldering rafters fell on us both.

"How is he?"

"The doctors are with him now."

"Call me back when you know more. In the meantime, I'll see what kind of help I can get to you and how fast."

"Hughes is on his way."

"Like he'd be any help," Deck muttered before ending the call.

"Dammit!" I said after he rang off, wishing I'd told him the phone he'd called me on wasn't mine.

I walked in the direction of the entrance to the emergency room. "Sorry, I had another call come in. Um, they might try to ring me back," I said to the woman who'd brought me the mobile.

"It's fine. It's my personal. Hang onto it as long as you need. I'm on shift another seven hours."

"You're sure?"

When she waved her hand and nodded, I went back to where the doctors were with Smoke.

"How is he?" I asked when they came out of the room.

"Not as bad as it looks. He suffered some second-degree burning but minimally. We'll keep our eye on him for a couple of hours, and then he can go home."

Home? Second-degree burns? I pushed open the door and sat down in the chair where I'd been earlier. "Hey," I said when he opened his eyes.

"Hey."

"Feeling no pain, are you?" I said when he smiled.

"I don't know why you kept saying no to this stuff."

When he turned his hand over, I rested my palm on his.

"Smoke, I—"

"You're mad at me."

"Mad? It's a bit more complicated than that."

"It always has been between us. Siren, I—"

I interrupted him like he had me. "There will be plenty of time to talk later. Now you should rest."

He closed his eyes for a few moments and then opened them again. "I'm afraid that when I wake up, you'll be gone."

"I'm not going anywhere, and if I do, it'll only be for a few minutes."

"Promise?"

"I promise." When Smoke closed his eyes again, mine filled with tears. Given my memory was back, for the most part at least, I could say with some certainty that I'd never seen Smoke as vulnerable as he was just now.

I thought back to when it was me lying in a hospital bed and Smoke sitting by my side. *Jaysus,* I'd asked the man to hold me! I stifled a laugh at the memory of the look on his face. It made so much more sense now that I could recall what our relationship had been like before I was shot. And yet, Smoke had been kind to me. He'd taken care of me. He'd even brought me to his ranch in the States.

None of that changed the conversation I'd heard between him and Decker, but as I'd said to him, there'd be time for us to talk later. For now, I would care for him as he had for me.

I traced the lines of his palms with my index finger, remembering how good those hands felt on my body. I leaned down and placed a kiss where my finger had been. Yes, things between us were complicated. And like Mr. O'Brien had said, there was a fine line between love and hate. While I could remember exactly what hating Smoke felt like, I also knew how it felt to love him.

# 27

*Smoke*

"Mr. Torcher, time to wake up," I heard a voice say.

"Go away," I grumbled without opening my eyes. I was having the most amazing dream about Siren, and I did not want it to end.

"I need to go over your discharge instructions with you, Mr. Torcher."

I felt a hand on my leg. "Come on, Smoke, when she's finished, I can get you out of here."

I opened one eye and saw Siren's beautiful face. Was I still dreaming?

"He's groggy from the pain medication," the sterner-voiced woman said. I looked up at her and decided to close my eyes again. I could hear her reviewing my discharge instructions with Siren, and part of me was afraid to hope she'd be the one caring for me.

"There's analgesic in the bandages. Do you have to go far?"

"About two hours."

"It should last longer than that, and he isn't due for pain meds for another four."

I drifted off when the nurse talked more about the bandages and changing them.

"Mr. Torcher, time for you to go."

I opened my eyes and glared at the woman.

"Oh, my. I'm glad you aren't my ward."

"That's his nice face," I heard Siren say to the woman.

Another man came in to help me off the gurney and over to a wheelchair. "I'd not recommend sitting back if you can help it," he said in a soft voice.

I took his advice and when I sat, leaned forward.

"Where are we going?" I asked when Siren and the same man helped me to the back passenger door of the car.

"To Waterford. I've made arrangements for a place we can stay tonight, at least."

"Why am I sitting back here?"

"Because you can lie down."

"No." I opened the front passenger door instead.

"So *feckin'* stubborn," she muttered, getting in beside me.

"If I was as stubborn as you seem to think I am, I'd insist on driving."

Siren laughed.

"Come here," I said, motioning her closer.

"What?"

"Just come here."

"I am here."

I reached out and grasped the back of her neck, pulling her so I could touch her lips with mine.

"What was that all about?" she asked when I released her.

"Later, when these meds wear off, I won't have the balls to do that."

"I know you better than that, Smoke. You have the balls—"

I kissed her again. I couldn't help it. I'd missed the feel of her lush lips, her soft tongue, her naked body against mine so fucking much.

"If you want me to stop doing that, you best not say another word about my balls, Siren."

By the time we turned down the residential street in Waterford where Siren said she'd arranged for us to stay, I was wishing I'd stretched out in the backseat like she suggested, even if the width of the car would've meant I'd have to bend my knees practically up to my chin.

"Whose place is this?" I asked when I saw lights on inside.

"My uncle's. Well, he's not really my uncle, but that's what I've called him most of my life."

The front door opened, and an older man walked toward us. "Can I help?" he asked.

"Uncle Gene, this is Smoke. If you'll get on one side, I'll be on the other."

They each took an arm and helped me inside. At first, I thought about telling them I was fine on my own, but after a couple of steps, I realized how light-headed I felt.

They didn't stop until they'd reached a door that led to a bedroom.

"Shannon, that's my neighbor, came over and helped me get the room ready for him. Fresh sheets and all."

"Thank you, Uncle Gene," said Siren, sitting beside me when I lay down.

"There's water on the bureau. The toilet is right across the hallway. Shannon also brought over some soup for when you're hungry."

"Smoke, do you want some soup?" Siren asked.

"Sleep," I mumbled.

"I'll leave you be," said Siren's uncle, or whoever he was.

When I felt Siren stand, I reached out and grabbed her wrist. "Don't leave."

"You need your rest. I'll just be in the other room."

"Don't leave," I repeated.

She sat back down. "Is this how it's going to be, then? You'll expect me to do your bidding? Be at your beck and call?"

"I want you next to me." I groaned when I tried to turn from my stomach to my side.

"Where is Maureen with that syringe full of pain medicine when you need her?" Siren muttered.

"I don't like her."

Siren stood again, and I grabbed her leg. "For crying out loud, I'm just getting a pill."

I could hear water being poured into a glass.

"Open," she said. "Stick out your tongue." She put a pill on it. "Now, drink." She brought the glass to my lips.

When I swallowed the pill, she set the glass on the table and stretched out beside me. "Tell me why you don't like Maureen."

"She helped you leave."

"Smoke…"

"Look at me, Siren."

She turned so she was facing me.

"Why did you leave like that?"

"There'll be time for us to talk about that later."

I shook my head. "That's what you said before. It's later. Talk."

"Admit it, Smoke. You were glad I left."

"Not true."

"Don't lie."

It was a struggle to keep my eyes open, but I was determined to have this conversation. "I'm not lying."

She tried to get up, but this time, I put my arm around her waist. It hurt like hell when I did, but I couldn't let her leave. I was too afraid I'd never see her again.

"Not lying," I repeated.

"I heard you."

She heard me? "What are you talking about?"

She let out a heavy sigh. "Talking to Decker."

"When?"

"Before I left."

It was getting as hard to talk as it was to keep my eyes open.

"Go to sleep, Smoke." When she ran her fingers through my hair, I couldn't fight it any longer.

It took me a minute to figure out where I was when I opened my eyes and light was streaming in through the bedroom window.

My body was stiff from sleeping in the same position all night, and my neck ached when I tried to turn it when I heard the door open.

"You're awake," said Siren's uncle who really wasn't her uncle. What the hell was his name? I couldn't remember.

"Where's Siren?"

"Siren? You mean Siobhan? She's just in the other room, on the phone."

I nodded and closed my eyes. "I need the bathroom."

"Let me get some help."

He rushed off before I could stop him. I shifted my body until I was close to the edge of the bed, bent my waist, and tried to sit up.

"Hang on, let me help you."

"Hughes? What are you doing here?"

"I drove down to Kinsale last night. Took me a *fecking* long time to locate the two of you."

I had a lot of questions, to most of which I didn't really care what the answers were. "Listen, Hughes, I gotta take a piss." He helped me up from the bed and held my arm. "I can walk, dammit."

"The ogre is finally awake," I heard Siren say from down the hall as I closed the bathroom door behind me.

When I came out, I didn't see Hughes, but Siren was standing across the hallway.

"How are you feeling?" she asked at the same time she handed me a pill and a glass of water.

"Like a burning building fell on top of me. How about you? I had to have hurt you when I landed on top of you."

"Come on," she said, taking my arm and leading me back into the bedroom.

"Siren? You didn't answer me."

"I'm fine, Smoke. A little sore is all."

"I'm sorry."

"Don't be sorry for saving my life, you *eejit*." She gently helped me back onto the bed and then walked around to lie next to me.

"Your uncle…what's his name?"

"Gene O'Brien."

"Right. He said you were on the phone."

"I had a few calls to make."

"Anything I need to know about?"

"I called to see how Jimmy Mallory was."

"And?"

"It's a miracle, but he's alive."

"He's the shop owner."

"The former shop. Not much left of it."

"I can't believe you went in there after him."

"It's what we're trained to do, Smoke. I couldn't just stand there and do nothing."

"There were firefighters there. Why didn't you tell them to go in."

She shrugged. "I just reacted."

"I could've lost you. I'd—"

"Smoke. Don't."

"Don't what?"

"Don't act like this is more than it is."

"What does that mean?"

"It means I know we were never what I thought we were. Not before, and not now."

I wanted to argue with her, tell her I wanted us to be more, wanted us to be together, but she was right. The reasons we'd never be a good fit hadn't changed.

"I have a house in Dublin. It's a shorter drive than from Kinsale to here. Do you think you'd be up for it?"

"Siren, you don't have to—"

She sat up and turned her back to me. "When you're able to travel, you can go wherever you'd like. Just allow me to help you like you helped me. Could you please just do that?"

"Yes."

She looked over her shoulder at me. "Good."

Since Hughes' car was quite a bit bigger than Siren's, I rode with him and, this time, agreed to stretching out in the back seat. There was really no way to strap me in, so Siren insisted we stop so she could buy pillows to stuff around me. Had I known that's why we were stopping or what her intentions were, I wouldn't have allowed it. On the other hand, this was Siren I was talking about. It wasn't like I'd ever had much say about what she did or didn't do.

"She drives like a damn bat out of hell," muttered Hughes.

"You got that right. A blind one at that."

He laughed.

"Smoke, you know it isn't going to be possible for me to keep Siren's condition a secret forever."

I shifted so I was sitting up. "What do you mean?"

"The head injury."

"The doctors in Asheville said there was no medical reason for her amnesia. Now that her memory is back, I don't see what the issue is."

"Her memory isn't back."

"Of course it is."

He shook his head. "That's why she's on leave—not that I told Byrne that."

"But that's why she left the States and returned to Ireland." Wasn't it? I vaguely remembered her saying something about overhearing me before I fell into a pain-medicine-induced deep sleep.

"It looks like you," I said when Hughes helped me inside Siren's house when she arrived a few minutes after we did.

"What's that mean?"

I stepped closer to her. "Warm, loving, never argumentative, stubborn, or belligerent."

"Very funny," she muttered.

"How did we arrive before you?" asked Hughes. "You were flying ahead of us."

"I had to stop." She held up what looked like a burner phone.

"Right. This brute crushed yours." Hughes pointed his thumb at me.

"He was saving my life," Siren mumbled. "You need to sit before you fall," she said to me. "Or would you prefer to lie down?"

She was close enough that I could grasp her arm. I pulled her closer and leaned in. "If you'll be in bed next to me, I'd much prefer it."

Siren rolled her eyes. "Pain meds."

We both looked in that direction when there was a knock at the door.

"I'll get it," said Hughes.

"What are you doing here?" I asked Casper when she raced inside and then abruptly stopped.

"I heard you almost died yesterday," she said, glaring at Siren.

"That still doesn't explain why you're here," said Siren, sending the nasty look back to her.

"Decker asked me to come. He's on his way too."

"Jesus, Mary, and Joseph," I heard Siren mumble. "It's a *feckin'* second-degree burn." She threw up her hands and went up the staircase.

"Excuse me," I said, following her. "What's going on?" I asked when I found her sitting on the edge of a bed with her back to the door.

"Nothing."

I went and sat beside her. "People don't generally rush out of a room over nothing."

"It's my house. I'll do what I want."

"Siren, look at me."

She shook her head.

"Please."

"They think I can't take care of you."

"I'm sure that isn't the case."

"Your precious Invincibles arrive within forty-eight hours and…"

"And what?"

"Nothing." She tried to stand, but I wouldn't let her.

"And what?" I repeated.

"Just go ahead and leave."

"Huh?"

"She's here to take you back to the States, so just leave. You'll be better off there anyway."

"Casper's on assignment in France. The same mission I was on. That's the only reason she's here."

"The two of you are working together?"

I shook my head. "Same op, but not together."

She slowly turned her head and studied me with one eyebrow raised.

"There's no reason for you to be jealous of Casper."

"You *feckin' eejit.*"

When she stood, I snaked an arm around her waist and pulled her onto my lap. "I'll ask her to leave."

"Just go with her."

I nuzzled her neck. "You owe me."

"I *what?*"

"All that time I took care of you. It's only fair."

"You hired a nurse."

She shuddered when I kissed her neck right below her ear. "There were other ways I took care of you, Siren. Admit it."

"Stop it," she murmured with no conviction whatsoever.

I reached up and circled her nipple with the tip of my finger through her sweater.

"Smoke," she groaned.

"Yeah?" I squeezed her breast. "I'm going to take care of you now, Siren."

She shook her head. "You can't."

"Of course I can." I cupped her mound with my palm.

"Your friend is downstairs," she murmured.

"So is yours. In fact, at one time, he was your lover. I'm the one who should be jealous."

"That was a long time ago."

"Prove it."

Her hooded eyes opened wide. "How?"

"Take your clothes off."

"*Now?* You're—"

"Do it, Siren. Let me see you naked." I let her stand, anxious to see if she'd walk out of the room or do as I asked. "Good girl," I said when she pulled her sweater over her head. "Now the pants."

She pointed to her bra.

"Leave it on."

She shimmied her jeans over her hips and pushed them to the floor.

"On the bed. Spread your legs for me."

"Smoke—"

"Do it, Siobhan."

I turned so my body was facing hers and put one of her legs across my lap and the other behind me. I ran one finger through her glistening folds, pressed my thumb against her clit, thrust two fingers inside her, and groaned. Siren's eyes met mine.

"There can be no pain with this much pleasure." As much as I wanted to replace my fingers with my throbbing cock, I knew that would be pushing my tolerance too far. Plus, this was me taking care of Siobhan. I had to taste her, though. I withdrew my hand and brought it to my mouth. Siren's body writhed on the bed. "Feeling empty, sweetheart?"

She nodded.

"Tell me what you need."

She grabbed my hand and brought it back to her pussy. I followed her gaze to the door of the bedroom I'd forgotten was open. I stood and shut it, making sure it was locked.

God, I wanted to fuck her. It was more than a want; I had to fuck her. I stalked back over to the bed and settled my body between her legs.

"Smoke, we can't—"

I might pay for this later, but it would be worth it. I was inside her with a single, hard thrust. "Put your legs around me."

"You're crazy," she moaned, but she did it. I was deeper this way. I could pleasure us both with less movement. I braced my body on my arms and rotated my hips.

I stilled when the realization hit me that I wasn't wearing a condom. I looked into Siren's eyes. "Birth control?"

"I'm on the pill," she said, grinding against me and then thrusting her hips, increasing the tempo until I rammed against her. I squeezed out every ounce of our pleasure before separating my body from hers. Siren rolled out from under me, and I lowered myself, face first, to the mattress. I felt a dip and then her body next to mine. Her leg was across my thighs, and I could feel her wet pussy against my hip. I didn't care what kind of pain I might be in when my brain finally registered it. Being inside Siren's steamy, hot body was worth it, especially when I felt her tongue trailing down my arm.

# 28



Smoke's cheek rested against the pillow, and I let my gaze linger on his face while he slept. Leave it to him to insist we have sex the day after burning rafters fell on him, singeing his flesh. He had to be in pain, yet he was able to sleep through it.

I heard noises from downstairs and wondered if Decker had arrived. I knew I should get up, put my clothes back on, and go check, but I didn't want to leave Smoke's side. I bent my neck and ran the tip of my tongue over the outline of the tattoo on his shoulder. It was of a bird in flight. A small bird. I wondered what its significance was as I studied the other ink that adorned his skin.

There were so many things I didn't know about Smoke. I wondered if there was anyone he revealed himself to more than superficially.

I remembered Ms. Wynona saying there was always a war waging inside of him. Why was that? What demons had started that war? Would I ever know?

Would he soon leave to return to America while I stayed here in Ireland?

When melancholia overcame me, I eased my body from the bed, put on my clothes, and crept out of the room. As I came down the stairs, three sets of eyes turned and looked up at me.

"Decker," I said, meeting his gaze first.

"How are you, Siren?"

"I've been better, but I've also been worse."

"How's Smoke?"

"Resting now." I walked over to where he, Casper, and Hughes were seated at my dining table. I pulled out the fourth chair and sat. "What's your plan?"

"What do you mean?"

"The reason you're all here."

"Siren, we—"

"I asked Decker." I didn't bother looking at Casper when she spoke. While I'd never had anything against her before, I didn't like that she came to my house uninvited.

"Will you excuse us?" he said to Hughes.

My boss pushed back and stood, but I knew he didn't like being asked to leave.

"You, too, Casper," Deck added.

The two of them went out the front door.

"What's your take on Hughes?" he asked once the door closed behind them.

"Meaning?"

"Do you trust him?"

"I do."

Decker nodded. "How are you feeling?"

"Back to normal, for the most part."

"What does that mean?"

"My memory is back." I flexed my hand. "No issues with movement."

"What's your plan?"

"I asked you a question, Decker, and you've yet to answer it."

"It depends on what you're going to do."

I sat back in my chair. "I don't know."

"Are you going back to IMI?"

"Why wouldn't I?"

He shrugged. "I thought maybe you were ready to branch out on your own."

"And what, join up with you?"

"Maybe."

"I'm not sure Smoke would like that."

Decker stretched his arms above his head and then leaned forward, resting his elbows on the table. "What makes you say that?"

"Don't think you can play with me, Decker. I heard your conversation with Smoke."

"Which one was that?"

I stood and walked over to the front window, surprised to see Hughes and Casper sitting in his car, having what looked like an animated conversation. Casper had a smile on her face, not something I'd seen very often. Rory was smiling too.

"Siren?"

"It doesn't matter, Deck. My memory is back. I know that Smoke and I were never together." What I hadn't figured out was why my brain had gone there in the first place. We'd had one night of drunken sex, yet for some inexplicable reason, my mind believed we were in love. *Jaysus*. Nothing could've been further from the truth.

"He loves you," said Decker, as though he was reading my mind.

I burst out laughing. "No. He doesn't." I tapped my temple with my fingertip. "I told you, I remember everything."

He shook his head. "You must not."

"Stop this, Ashford," I snapped. "There is nothing between Smoke and me. Nothing. And there never will be." Deck turned his head, and I followed his gaze. Smoke stood on the stairs, gripping the railing and staring at me. He looked hurt, but that was ridiculous. I'd heard him. As soon as my memory came back, he said he'd make sure we never saw each other again.

"Hey, Deck," Smoke said, his eyes finally leaving mine. "Glad you're here."

Decker got up and met Smoke at the bottom step. "How are you doing?"

Smoke turned his head back to me. "Ready to go home."

# 29

*Smoke*

I had no idea what the beginning of Siren's conversation with Decker sounded like, but I'd heard the end loud and clear. She said there was nothing between us and there never would be. I'd endured indescribable pain to make love to her only a few minutes earlier, and yet she just said there was nothing between us and there never would be.

"Deck, Smoke and I need to talk."

My friend turned to me, and I nodded once. "Don't go too far."

"Copy that."

"Where are Casper and Hughes?"

Siren put her hands on her hips. "Why?"

I shook my head. "Just curious," I mumbled.

"They're outside. Talking. She looks quite happy, in fact. Shall I go and fetch her for you?"

"Stop it."

"Something's just occurred to me."

I rested my hip against the kitchen counter top, wondering how much longer I could remain standing. "What is that, Siren?"

"That's why you were so anxious to be rid of me once my memory returned, you and Casper—"

I stalked over to her and got in her face. "Quit it. There's nothing between Casper and me. There never has been and there never will be. But I'm curious why you care when you just said there'll never be anything between you and me."

"You aren't the only one who overheard a conversation, Smoke."

I was beginning to feel lightheaded. "I need to sit." She was furious with me; she had been often enough that I knew the signs. However, she still helped me over to a chair. "Sit down."

"No."

"Dammit, Siren. Sit the fuck down."

"Don't talk to me that way, Smoke! If that's how you've talked to the other women in your life, then I can't say I'm surprised you're alone."

I lowered my head. That one hurt.

"I'm sorry," she murmured and took a seat.

"So am I."

"This is what we do, isn't it? We hurt each other?"

"Not always."

"No? I don't remember it being any other way."

"Maybe not before you were shot." She tried to stand, but I captured her wrist. "Before you were shot," I repeated. "And then things changed."

"Bullshit," she spat, wrenching her wrist from my grasp. "It didn't change; you just lied."

"I don't know what you thought you heard, but whatever it was, you took it out of context."

She walked over to the window, folded her arms, and then turned back to look at me. "Like you took my words out of context? A few minutes ago, you told Decker you were ready to leave."

As much as I wanted to, I didn't have the strength to get up and walk over to her. "Siren, please." I held my hand out to her, but she shook her head.

"Do you have any idea how devastated I was that day?"

"Tell me."

She took a deep breath and looked out the window. "Decker asked what you were going to do."

"About what?"

"Me."

"And what did I say?"

"That as soon as my memory came back, you'd make sure no one ever teamed you up with me again."

"There was more to it than that."

"That was the only part that mattered."

"And what did I say next?"

Siren was looking out the window; her head was cocked.

"What?" I asked.

"Uncle Gene is here. He looks upset." She raced to the front door, and again, as much as I wanted to follow, I didn't have the strength.

"Come inside and sit down," I heard her say. When he came through the door, his face was ashen. I moved the chair with my foot and motioned for him to sit.

"Tell me what's happened," said Siren, sitting on the other side of him.

"I went to see Jimmy."

She reached out and took his hand. "How is he?"

"Not well. He asked me to go to the shop and find the safe. When I got there, it was gone. When I told him, he went nuts, said they were going to kill him. He left the hospital, and no one knows where he is. This is all my fault."

I looked up and saw Casper, Hughes, and Decker standing just inside the front door.

"Why would someone kill him over a safe?" Gene asked, looking between Siren and me.

"It's what's in it," she murmured, and her eyes met mine. "Something tells me it isn't the Irish Crown Jewels."

I had to agree.

She stood. "We need to find him."

"But where would he go?" Gene asked.

I looked over at Decker, who was already searching his computer.

"I can't just sit here. I need to do *something,*" Siren muttered.

"Let's craft a plan before anyone does anything." Deck was looking at something on the laptop he pulled out of a bag. "There are some other things I need." He got up, went out the front door, and motioned to Hughes, who followed.

Siren looked up at the clock hanging on the kitchen wall. "You need a pain pill, and I have to change your bandages."

"Give me the pill. The other can wait."

Siren shook her head. "You'll get an infection."

"It sounds like you care."

"I do care about you, Smoke," she muttered. "It's you who doesn't."

"Wrong. And when this crowd disperses, I'm going to tell you what you didn't hear me say to Decker that day."

"What about me?" Deck asked, coming back inside with Hughes trailing behind him. The two of them proceeded to walk the rooms of the house, most likely looking for listening devices.

"He thinks my house is bugged?" Siren whispered.

"Precaution."

Deck came back to where we waited. "We're good."

"If the safe is gone, I don't understand why Jimmy is so terrified that someone is going to kill him. Whoever took it, got what they wanted," said Gene.

"He knows its contents."

"Wait," said Siren, looking at me. "How did you know I was in Kinsale?"

Deck looked up from his computer. "That was me."

"And me," added Casper.

"Why?" Siren looked at Casper specifically.

"Someone at Interpol was tracking you."

"Who?"

Every head in the room turned to look at Hughes, except Siren, who was looking at me.

"What's going on?" she asked.

"*Jaysus,*" muttered Hughes. "It was me."

"You were tracking me?"

Hughes shook his head. "I tipped the bastard off."

Siren's frustration was nearing a boiling point. I reached over and rubbed her shoulder.

"You need a pain pill." She raced upstairs, and I let her go.

"It's Byrne, isn't it?" Hughes asked in a hushed tone.

Casper nodded.

"What did you tell him?" I asked.

"That Siren was off looking for the Irish Crown Jewels."

"What else?"

"I mentioned she was going so far as trying to meet with Mallory's grandson."

"When was this?" Deck asked.

Hughes pulled out his phone, and Casper looked at the screen.

"The day Byrne sent the order for her to be tracked," she answered.

"Byrne?" Siren asked, coming down the stairs. "He was the one tracking me?"

I nodded.

She handed me the pill before getting a glass of water.

"I think we can all agree that whatever is in that safe has nothing to do with the missing crown jewels."

No one spoke, but everyone in the room nodded in my direction.

"Who do you think took it?" Siren asked.

"Whoever Byrne sent to Kinsale," answered Casper.

"And you followed," Siren whispered.

"That's right."

"We need to rethink our base," Decker muttered.

"I can make arrangements—"

Deck interrupted Hughes. "Somewhere that IMI can't track us."

"Look, if you want me out—"

"I didn't say that. I said we need to find somewhere *IMI* can't track us. If you can't work within those parameters, leave." Decker looked from Hughes, who didn't make a move to walk out, to Casper. "What's Byrne's twenty?"

"The quarterly meetings concluded last week, so he should be back in Dublin."

"Then, you stay put for now."

"Copy that."

"The safe is likely still in Ireland."

"You're probably right, Smoke," said Deck. "Either still somewhere in Kinsale, if not already in Dublin."

Hughes was studying something on his phone.

"What's up?" I asked.

He looked first at O'Brien and then at me. He walked over and handed me the phone; Siren looked over my shoulder.

"Have a seat, Gene," I said.

"They found Jimmy, didn't they?"

"They did."

Gene put his head in his hands.

"We need to get Uncle Gene to a safe location," suggested Siren. "I have to change Smoke's bandages before I can leave."

"You aren't going anywhere," said Deck, packing up his stuff.

"What do you mean?"

"The two of you are staying put."

I took one look at Siren's face and laughed, which made both she and Decker glare at me.

"Sorry, man, but if you think you're gonna get away with that shit, you don't know a thing about Siren."

Evidently, that was the wrong thing to say to Decker. On the other hand, Siren was beaming at me, and *that* was all I cared about.

# 30

*Siren*

Endless questions raced through my head. What in hell was in that safe, and why in God's name had I set this chain of events in motion? What had started as a silly whim to assuage my boredom, resulted in a man's death.

What was Byrne's involvement in all of this? I couldn't bear the idea that he had anything to do with Jimmy's death. It was Byrne who'd recruited me for IMI in the first place. I had to admit I'd often wondered why. As a candidate, I hadn't exactly stood out among my peers.

"Uncle Gene? Does the name Daniel Byrne mean anything to you?"

"Just wondering."

"What are you thinking?" Smoke asked me.

I motioned for him to follow me upstairs and then thought better of it. "Are you able?"

He didn't answer right away. "Not that I know of," he finally said. "Why, lass?"

"I'm steadier now that the pain meds have kicked in."

Instead of leading, I followed.

"If you're looking for a command performance, I gotta tell you, I don't think I'm up for it yet."

I rolled my eyes. "Yes, Smoke, I can't keep my hands off of you; that's why I asked you upstairs."

"Why did you?"

"I'm trying to connect the dots."

He nodded.

"James Mallory Sr. worked for Arthur Vicars, the man responsible for safekeeping the jewels at the time of their disappearance. His son was one of my father's best friends."

Smoke raised a brow. "Your father?"

"Right. I'll come back around to that. Anyway, Jimmy Mallory is deceased, and the man who is the current head of Irish Military Intelligence is having me tracked, and sent someone to Kinsale where Jimmy, a now-missing safe, and I all were. And finally, we all agree that none of this has anything to do with my original subject of interest—the missing Irish Crown Jewels."

"Can you circle back to your father?"

I told Smoke about meeting Gene O'Brien in the Waterford Cemetery while I was visiting my mother's grave. "I was so frustrated at not being able to remember anything of her other than bits and pieces."

"You had no other memories of your mother?"

I knocked my head with my knuckles. "Amnesia, remember?"

"But your memory was back."

"What would make you think that?"

"That's why you left the ranch."

I shook my head. "No, Smoke. I've told you, I left the ranch because of the conversation I overheard between you and Decker."

"What about now?"

"Do you mean my memory?"

He nodded.

"I believe the trigger was being flattened on the floor of a burnt-out building and having a ceiling fall on me."

"That's when it came back?"

"So it seems."

"Come here."

I walked closer to Smoke, and he wrapped me in his arms. "I need to tell you what you didn't hear that day."

"It isn't important."

He cupped my cheek with his palm. "It's the most important thing of all."

We both sat on the bed. Smoke kept my hands clasped in his. "You said the last thing you heard was me saying something about our not working together again once your amnesia went away."

"That's right."

"What happened next?"

"What do you mean?"

"Decker and I were still talking."

"Oh. I left."

Smoke took a deep breath and let it out slowly. I thought he was about to speak, but instead, he kissed me. He cupped my face with his hands, and his mouth made love to mine. His touch was soft and gentle, slow and oh, so sweet that I felt my body and my heart melting into him. He pushed me back onto the bed and looked into my eyes.

"How does it make you feel when I kiss you?"

I turned away.

"I'll tell you what I feel," he said, gently turning my head back toward him. "I feel everything."

I smiled. "Vague."

"Things I've never felt before."

"Such as?"

"Hope."

"What are you hopeful for?"

Smoke laughed. "You aren't going to make this easy on me, are you?"

"You could just tell me what you and Decker said after I left."

"Okay." Smoke took another deep breath. "I said that I was falling…that…you know…um…that I…uh…love you."

"Did that hurt?"

Smoke put his hand on my neck. "No, the painful thing is that your response is to ask me that."

"You asked me what I felt when you kissed me. Couldn't you tell? Can't you tell when I look into your eyes?"

"Siren—"

"When I woke with amnesia, my subconscious was certain I loved you and you loved me. Why do you think that is?"

"I don't know."

"I think it's because deep down, we did love each other. Deep down, we both knew that, even though our conscious minds fought against it, resisted, and denied it. There were parts of our souls that knew from the very beginning."

"How do you feel about me, Siobhan?"

"You make me feel things I've never felt before, either."

"Such as?"

"Dependence."

Smoke closed his eyes, took yet another deep breath, and opened them. "That doesn't sound like a good thing."

"For someone like me, it is. I feel safe with you, even when I'm feeling my most vulnerable. When Uncle Gene first told me he knew my father, I wished so much that you were there beside me. I imagined you were, and that was what gave me the strength to let him tell me more."

"Please," he whispered.

"I love you, Smoke. I can't deny it. I don't want to deny it."

He rested his head on his hand. "We're a pair, aren't we? Took that long for either of us to be able to say it."

"What's going to happen, Smoke?"

"Between us?"

"Yes."

"I'm a lot older than you are, Siren."

"That's the least of my concerns."

"It shouldn't be. In ten years, you'll still be younger than I am now. Think about that."

I shrugged. As virile as he was, he'd likely outlive me. "What about our jobs?" I had this house that I was never at, and according to Ms. Wynona, he was never at his ranch either. How could we ever be together if neither of us managed to be home?

"We'd have to work hard to figure it out."

"I don't want to give up my work, Smoke."

"And I don't want you to."

"No one will guarantee we'll always work together."

"Nor do I think that's a good idea."

"Why not?"

Smoke laughed. "Don't get your hackles up. It's not what you're thinking."

"Then, what is it?"

"I'm not sure how effective I'd be."

"Because you'd be too worried about protecting me?"

"Hey, you got those bandages changed yet?" said Decker, pounding on the bedroom door.

"Give us another few minutes," I hollered back.

"Jesus Christ, we've got a damn..." muttered Decker, his voice trailing off.

I shifted out from under Smoke, stood, and picked up the medical supplies the hospital gave us when he was discharged.

"You sure you're up for this?" he asked.

"I can assure you, I've seen far worse."

"That's what I thought when the nurse in England warned me about how you'd look after your surgery."

"And?"

"It nearly broke my heart to see you lying in that bed with bandages on your head and monitors hooked up everywhere. The worst part was that they had you restrained. As soon as she left the room, I untied you."

"See, Smoke, you loved me then."

He nodded and then grimaced when I removed the bandages from his back.

# 31

*Smoke*

The obvious answer to what was in the safe was it contained evidence that would prove Byrne, and perhaps the other two men who worked for Interpol, was connected to the murder of agents around the globe. Either that or evidence of some other crime he'd committed. Why else would he or someone who worked for him kill Jimmy Mallory?

Siren still hadn't told me what she learned about her father or of the strange coincidence that he was friends with Jimmy's dad.

As hard as I tried not to move, when the cold analgesic on the replacement bandages hit my back, I flinched.

"Sorry," she mumbled.

"Siren, what about your father?"

She sat down on the bed, beside me. "Turns out I followed in his footsteps."

I couldn't hide the fact her news stunned me. "He's with IMI?"

"Was."

"What happened?"

"He lost his life while on an op searching for Veronica Guerin's killer."

"You were a baby."

"Not yet born is my understanding."

"That's why your mother didn't list him on your birth certificate."

"She feared some kind of retaliation."

"Do you remember her ever talking about him?"

"Never. They weren't married, although Uncle Gene said they intended to be." Siren startled when there was another knock on the door. I stood and opened it.

"I think I know where the safe is," said Deck. "We're moving out."

"I'm coming with you."

Decker looked from Siren to me.

"If you think I'm going to try to talk her out of it, you're wrong."

"We don't have time to move Gene to a safe house," he said.

I watched the struggle play out on Siren's face. "I'm not decrepit yet," I said, nudging her. "Go if that's what you want to do."

"I do."

Her trust in me mirrored my trust in her. I don't know if she saw it that way, but I did.

I followed them downstairs and walked Siren to the door. "See you on the other side."

She stood on her tiptoes and kissed me.

"The two of you remind me of her parents," said Gene once the door was closed.

"Yeah? Siobhan told me that you were able to tell her about her father."

"Aye. They burned hot as coal, those two."

I laughed. "Good way to put it."

"Their love was clear as could be to everyone else, just like yours and Siobhan's."

I don't know what compelled me to confide in Gene, but I did. "I do love her."

"Does she know that?"

"She does. I know she loves me. The question is, can it be enough? In our line of work, well, you know what happened to her father."

"Some said at the time that he was killed by the wrong side."

I raised my head. "Friendly fire?"

"Is that what they call it, then?" Gene shook his head. "Friendly, even though it killed the man."

I'd heard about too much of it as of late between Beau Rey and the agents killed around the world, murdered by the very men who'd put them in harm's way in the first place. My assumption was there'd been accidental deaths caused by those fighting on the same side since the beginning of time.

However, my gut told me that Beau's death was no accident, friendly fire or otherwise. The same was true for every agent who may have died by an order given by Daniel Byrne, Boris Antonov, or Kim Ha-joon.

Siren, Casper, Decker, and Hughes hadn't been gone more than a few minutes when Gene dozed off in his chair. I went to look around Siren's house. Yeah, I was snooping, but she loved me, so maybe she'd consider it as me just trying to learn more about her.

I wasn't necessarily a messy guy; I wasn't home enough to make a big mess. But, Siren? She was a goddamn neat freak. Every drawer I opened in her kitchen was perfectly organized. She didn't even have a junk drawer that I could find. Who didn't have a fucking junk drawer?

I went upstairs to the master bedroom and found the same thing. Nothing out of place in her closet or bathroom drawers and cabinets. Even the clothes in her dresser were perfectly folded. It was beginning to freak me out. The woman had to have a room in her house that wasn't straight out of a *Better Homes and Gardens'* photoshoot.

I traipsed from room to room on a mission to find even one thing out of place. When I got to the back of the house, I found another staircase. I climbed the steps and came to a single door at the top. I opened it, thinking maybe Siren kept boxes of crap up here. Instead, the attic room was empty.

"Maybe she has OCD," I muttered to myself, walking back down. I checked the time as I walked past the master bedroom. I had two hours before I was supposed to take another pain pill, not that I was feeling much pain. The only thing I felt was bored.

How many more years would it be before I was like Gene? Falling asleep in an easy chair in the middle of the afternoon?

I remembered seeing a workout room on the second level and thought briefly about trying to get some exercise. I decided against it, knowing that if I didn't let my back heal, it would only add to the number of days I felt antsy enough to want to pull my hair out.

I checked the time again. It had only been twenty minutes since Siren and the others left. This didn't bode well for the future. Would I feel this way every time she was on a mission and I wasn't?

I walked down the main stairs and noticed Gene was no longer sitting in the chair. Maybe he was in the bathroom. That was another thing. Didn't men have to take a piss more often the older we got?

I decided to make some lunch and was about to round the corner to the kitchen when I felt the muzzle of a gun press against my back.

In front of me sat Gene O'Brien, bound and gagged, with a gun pressed into his temple.

"Smoke," said Daniel Byrne. "How nice it is to see you again. Unfortunate circumstances, as they say."

"What the fuck, Byrne?" I motioned toward Gene, whose face was bright red; sweat ran down his forehead.

Whoever held the gun behind me, jammed the barrel harder into my back. The pain of it pressing against my burn was so intense, I almost passed out.

"What do you want?"

"I'd let ol' Gene here tell you, but since I've gagged him, he can't. He knows why I'm here, though. Don't ya, Gene?" The old man shook his head.

# 32

*Siren*

By the time we reached the location where Decker believed Byrne was with the safe, he was gone.

"We just missed him," he muttered into the headset to inform Casper and Hughes, who'd followed in Hughes' SUV. He pulled out his phone and punched the screen. "Goddamn motherfucker," he spat. "He's on his way to your place. *Move out.*"

I threw my car in reverse and sped away from the back of the barracks.

Whatever Byrne thought was in the safe, must not have been. Since he'd been tracking me, he either thought I had it or Gene did.

"You were able to track him."

"Hughes took care of it."

If anything would prove his loyalty wasn't with Byrne, that should've been it.

"How many have you got that you can trust for backup?" Decker asked Hughes through the headset.

"I've got four heading over now."

"That you trust?"

"Affirmative. I don't need to tell you there is a group inside IMI who believes Byrne is dirty."

My eyes opened wide. Why had I never heard this? Was it because those same people believed I'd be loyal to the man? Given he'd recruited me, I supposed that was a logical assumption. I'd also officially been "on loan" to MI6 for the last few months, even though the mission I'd been on was for the Invincibles. But regardless, I'd been out of touch with IMI.

"Pull over," said Deck. "I'll go in with Hughes and Casper. If Byrne is there, Smoke hasn't managed to neutralize him, or he would've been in contact. I want Byrne to think you're arriving on your own."

"Roger that." I pulled off into a parking lot.

"Hughes?" said Deck.

"Copy," I heard Casper respond at the same time Hughes pulled in behind me.

"What is it with IMI not giving proper response?" he asked, hitting the kill switch on his mic before he spoke.

"Hey, now."

"You're definitely the exception, Siren," he muttered before turning his mic back on. "Remove your headset."

"Why?"

"Because I asked you to," he answered without looking up at me. "Here." Decker handed me something flesh-colored and not much bigger than the head of a pin. "What is this?"

"Put it on the tip of your finger and then insert it as far as you can into your auditory canal. Casper?"

"Testing, test, test, test," I could hear her say inside my ear.

"Copy," I responded.

"Copy back," said Casper.

"You amaze me," I mumbled.

"Why, thank you," said Casper, although I was sure she knew I was speaking to Deck.

"By the way, no one outside of the Invincibles knows about this technology. Except you and now Hughes."

"Understood."

He showed me something on his phone. "Is this a back entrance to the complex?"

"Yes." I pointed where they could enter and park without being seen from my house.

"Wait for my signal," he said, climbing out. "Head out in five, and I'll see you on the other side."

"Roger that."

"We're in position," said Deck.

"Doppler indicates a count of six," Casper reported.

Smoke, Uncle Gene, Byrne, and the other three had to be muscle.

I was little, but that didn't mean I couldn't take even the biggest guys. It was all about where, when, and how I struck. Casper outweighed me by at least a stone and a half.

With the four agents Hughes had delivered from IMI, we had Byrne far outnumbered. It was just a matter of striking in such a way that the hostages—which we had to assume Smoke and Uncle Gene were—remained unharmed.

"Move out. We've got your six," said Decker.

"Roger that."

When I pulled up in front of my place, the first thing I noticed was one of the doors on Gene's car was partially ajar. Second, there were no other vehicles in sight.

When I walked inside the house, the first face I saw was Smoke's. He made brief eye contact, then his eyes went left.

"One, one, one, five," I whispered as quietly as I could without moving my lips.

"Siren," said Byrne, who stepped out from where Smoke had indicated at the same time another man approached from my right, frisked me, and took my weapons. "So glad you could join us."

"What are you doing here, and what in the hell is this?" I motioned with my hand toward Smoke and Gene, both of whom were gagged and bound to chairs.

Byrne smiled. "Don't play coy with me. You know very well that there's something I need your help with."

"There are far easier ways to ask. No need to hold my friends at gunpoint."

"So amusing," he said, motioning to a terrified-looking Gene. "Don't you find her amusing?" Byrne said to Smoke, whose only response was a growling sound that emanated from his throat. It got louder when Byrne put his arm around my shoulders.

"Have you ever wondered why I recruited you, Siren?"

I shook my head. "Never. Perfectly obvious to me. I was the best in my class."

Byrne laughed out loud. "Far from it. No, girl, it wasn't that you were the best or even in the top ninety percent of your class."

"Now you're just being unnecessarily mean."

He shook his head. "It was more that I had to keep my eye on you. I knew one day your curiosity would get the better of you, and then you'd lead me exactly where you have."

I saw the safe I'd seen in the back of the antique shop sitting on my dining room table. "Are you under the assumption I have the combination to that thing?"

His fingers dug into the back of my neck, and he brought his face close enough to mine that I could smell whiskey on his breath. "I've grown weary of your feeble attempts at humor. You know goddamn well what was in that safe, and it wasn't diamonds and emeralds. Now, tell me what you've done with it."

"I have no idea what you're talking about."

He moved his hand to the front of my throat and slowly tightened his grip. "Willing to die? And for what? Ancient history that no one gives a shit about?" He released my neck and shoved me. "Stupid girl. So much like your father." Byrne walked over, put his gun to Gene's head, and cocked it. "Not so brave with someone else's life. You have until the count of five to tell me where you hid it."

I crossed my arms in front of me. "You can count to three and kill him, and it won't change the fact I have no idea what you're talking about. I never saw inside the safe, and I certainly never took anything from it."

Byrne moved the gun from Gene's head and pointed it at me. "If that is the case, you are worthless to me."

From behind him, Gene began to thrash about in his chair, trying to scream through his gag. It sounded as though he was trying to say, "*I know.*"

"Untie him," I demanded.

Byrne backhanded me, and I fell against the wall of muscle standing at my back. "You don't make the rules."

Gene continued to thrash about to the extent that I feared the chair would topple over.

"For *feck's* sake," muttered Byrne. "Untie the gag." He motioned with his gun at me; the muscle shoved me at Gene.

"I know!" he screamed when I untied his gag. "I know where it is!"

"You better not be playing me, old man. If you are, I'll make your last day on earth a living hell of pain."

Gene frantically shook his head and looked at me.

"Your m-m-mother," he stammered. "The b-b-box."

"The box?"

Four things happened simultaneously. First, I realized which box Gene was talking about. Second, Byrne knew that I had. Third, when my eyes sought Smoke's, I noticed he'd worked himself free and was waiting for the right time to strike. And finally, I saw that Byrne's sloppiness in having his three goons on the inside rather than on the perimeter, meant Decker and the rest of our team had been able to get inside unnoticed.

While all eyes in the room remained focused on Gene and me, I saw Hughes creeping toward us in the hallway, along with Casper and Deck standing at the ready from two of the other rooms' doorways. I had no doubt the others were standing ready to burst through the front door the second I gave the signal.

My eyes met Smoke's one more time. He blinked thrice in rapid succession; I counted three seconds in my head and screamed, *"Now!"*

I dove, knocking Gene's chair to the ground and covering his body with mine like Smoke had done to me before the ceiling crashed down on us.

I closed my eyes tight as bullets flew all around us, and prayed.

# 33

*Smoke*

Within seconds, Byrne was dead, and so were the three men with him. I walked over and put my hand on Siren's back and knelt down beside her. "It's over," I said, easing her body from Gene's.

Casper untied him, and I pulled Siren into my arms.

"What happened?" she asked.

"They're all dead," I answered, knowing full well that wasn't what she meant.

"You got this?" Decker asked Hughes. When he gave a thumbs up, I escorted Siren out while Casper and Deck helped Gene.

"Hughes said there's a safe house close."

"There is," said Siren. "I can get us there."

While Byrne had been neutralized, there was still the question of the men he'd been working with. Until we knew exactly who they were, we weren't in any position to let our guard down.

I had, and that was what had let Byrne get the upper hand.

"Let it go for now," said Decker as I got in the back of the SUV behind Siren.

I knew I had to. If I didn't focus on the here and now, we could wind up in a worse situation than the one I'd landed Gene and I in. That didn't mean I could stop the mistakes I'd made from lingering in the back of my mind.

Siren sat between Gene and I and held his hand. Apart from her giving Casper directions to the safe house, we were all quiet on the drive. Each of us had our own experiences to process through before the hot-wash that would eventually come.

"How's your pain?" Siren whispered.

"Too much adrenaline to feel much of anything," I muttered without looking at her. She squeezed my thigh with her hand and rested her head on my shoulder. Was she trying to give me comfort, knowing that I recognized my fuck up as much or more than anyone else in the vehicle? Even Gene knew that because of me, he had almost lost his life. I'd been distracted; my head wasn't in the game; I didn't protect my asset.

We approached the safe house, waited while the garage door opened, and then pulled inside. Like when we'd left Siren's place, Decker and Casper helped Gene.

"Wait," said Siren, stopping me before we followed the others inside. She put her arms around me and rested her cheek on my chest. "I've never been so frightened in my life. Thank God you're okay."

Her words were meant to bring me comfort, but they did the opposite. She'd been frightened and worried because of me. Her head hadn't been in the right place, not that she'd done a single thing wrong. She'd handled herself like the professional she was—unlike me.

"Smoke?"

"Yeah," I mumbled, looking down at her.

"I love you."

"I love you too." I removed her hands from around my waist. "Let's get inside."

"Casper is working on Kim's and Antonov's twenty," said Decker. "Hughes is on his way here now." He looked at Siren. "The two of you will need to do an assessment of IMI agents." Deck turned to me. "We'll get a medic over here to assess your condition as well as Mr. O'Brien's."

"Not necessary. I'm fine."

Decker nodded.

"Both Kim and Antonov have been located. Kim is in his office at Interpol. Antonov is back in Moscow."

"Stay on them," said Deck. Casper nodded.

"What about the box?" asked Siren.

"You know what he was talking about?" Deck asked. She looked at O'Brien. "It's at my old house."

Gene nodded.

"The woman who owns it now tried to give it to me the day we first met in the cemetery, and I told her I'd come back for it." Siren turned to me; her eyes were scrunched. "I forgot."

I held my arms open, and she walked into them. "It's better that you did. If Byrne had found it at your house, both Gene and I would probably be dead."

Siren's shoulders began to shake. The adrenaline was wearing off, and she was crashing.

"Come here," I said, leading her down the hallway. I opened the first door I came to. It was a bathroom, so I went to the next. I led Siren in and over to the bed. "Lie down, kiddo."

"Will you hold me?"

"I will." I lay on my back and pulled her into my arms.

"Isn't that painful?"

"I'm fine," I muttered, stroking her hair. After a few minutes, she looked up at me.

"Tell me what you're thinking."

"How good you feel next to me."

She shook her head. "No, you're not. You're thinking you screwed up."

"I did screw up."

"What happened?"

I had my mind on her, not the job, but I wasn't about to say so. Nothing that had happened was her fault.

"Smoke?"

"I didn't do my job."

"Okay," she whispered, and I knew it meant she got that I didn't want to talk about it.

"Sounds like Hughes is here. We should get back out there."

Her arm tightened around my waist. "Another minute."

# 34

*Siren*

I told Smoke I'd never been more afraid in my life, but now that wasn't true. I was more afraid at this moment. He was pulling away from me, and I could feel it. He blamed himself for not protecting Gene and me. It hadn't been Smoke's job to look after me, but it had been with Gene. If I were in his shoes, I'd be retreating too. The difference was, I'd disappear into myself professionally. Smoke was pulling away on a personal level too. I knew exactly how he saw this playing out, and I had no intention of letting him.

It didn't matter what it took. I wasn't about to watch Smoke walk out of my life. I'd do whatever I had to, to make sure he stayed in it.

When Hughes and I finished assessing IMI's agent list, I looked around for Smoke. I found him back in the bedroom we'd been in, sitting on the edge of the bed, staring out the window.

"I need to go and get the box," I said, sitting beside him. "I want you to come with me."

Smoke's eyes met mine. "That isn't a good idea."

I nodded. "I'll wait until you're ready, then."

"Don't, Siren."

"Don't what?"

"Don't try to make this better for me. It isn't going to work. As soon as I'm no longer needed here, I'm taking leave and going home."

"I see."

"It's for the best, and we both know it."

"You wouldn't let me get away with this shit."

He didn't respond, so I stood.

*"Smoke, you wouldn't let me get away with this shit."* This time I shouted it at him.

"Stop it."

"The *feckin'* hell I will."

"You're outta your league, little girl. I got years on you, and I'm telling you to stand the fuck down."

"Kiddo, little girl—you don't think I see what you're doing? You think you can put *me* in my place? You think you can make me feel inferior because of my lack of experience compared to yours? You're dead wrong, *arsehole*."

Smoke stood, picked me up by the waist, moved me out of his way, and stalked out of the bedroom. I stayed right on his heels. Before we got more than a couple of steps down the hallway, he spun around on me and pointed his finger in my face. "Leave me the fuck alone," he seethed.

I had no intention of backing down and got right back in his face. "Never." I saw Decker approach from behind Smoke and shook my head. Casper was right behind him. "Stay out of this, the both of you. This is between Smoke and me." My eyes met Casper's; she smiled and nodded in what I could only assume was support. I turned my attention back to the man I loved. "If I screwed up, would you walk away from me?" I asked, keeping my voice soft. "Would you let me go if I felt like I needed to run away?" I took a deep breath. "Would you stop loving me, Smoke?"

His eyes bored into mine.

"Answer me, Smoke. Would you stop loving me?"

It took a long while before he responded, and even then, he didn't speak. His head moved from side to side, barely detectable.

"You wouldn't," I said for him. "I won't either." I took his hand and led him back into the bedroom, thankful he didn't resist. I closed the door behind us. I took another deep breath, knowing the ultimatum I was about to issue may end things between Smoke and me forever, but I had to do it.

"This is it, Smoke. Right here, right now. Either we're together or we're not. If we're together, it's forever."

The glimmer of a smile I saw in his eyes gave me hope.

"Answer me, dammit."

"I didn't hear a question."

"All right, then. You want it phrased as a question? Fine. I can do that. Broderick Smoke Torcher, will you marry me?"

His eyes opened wide. "*Marry* you?"

"That's right. Marry me. In sickness and in health. 'Til death do us part. All that jazz."

"When you put it like that…"

I gritted my teeth. "Yes or no, Smoke. Will you marry me?" He cupped my cheek with his palm, and I leaned into his hand. "Please say yes, Smoke."

"Yes, Siobhan Siren Gallagher, soon to be Torcher. I will marry you."

My eyes filled with tears as I pushed away the ramifications of what we'd both just said. I hadn't thought about anything other than spending the rest of my life with the man I loved, and that was exactly how it should be. We'd figure everything else out. Our jobs. Where we lived. None of that mattered compared to having Smoke in my life forever.

He brushed my tears away with this thumb and my lips with his. "You sure about this?" he asked, his forehead resting against mine.

"The only thing I've ever been as sure of was when I woke up in the hospital in London, looked into your eyes, and knew in my heart that I loved you and you loved me."

# 35

*Smoke*

*Married.* Siren and I were getting married. Instead of thinking it was ridiculous or even being terrified by it, it felt right. More right than anything in my life up to this point. And while it had been spur of the moment, fueled by the harrowing experience we'd shared, I knew, like she did, that it was real.

I smiled to myself, thinking that no proposal in the history of the universe could have been more appropriate for Siren and me. Of course she was the one to ask me. It was the way it was supposed to be. I would've wanted to marry her. There would've come a time I admitted it to myself, but it would have taken months, maybe even years, until I stopped trying to talk myself out of believing she'd want the same thing.

I let her lead me by the hand out to where Decker, Casper, Hughes, and Uncle Gene waited.

"We're getting married," Siren announced like she might have if she'd told them we were going out for lunch.

I looked at Casper and watched as her smiling eyes filled with tears. I dropped Siren's hand and walked over to her.

"Congratulations," she whispered, hugging me. "I would've had to kick your ass if you screwed things up with her."

"She'd never let me."

Casper laughed. "I believe it."

I turned around and saw Hughes hugging my future wife and knew he was as happy for us as Casper was.

"Hey, Gene," I said, resting my hand on his shoulder. He looked stunned. "You okay?"

He smiled. "You're a lucky man."

I nodded. "The luckiest."

"She reminds me of my Janie. She was incandescent. Her passion, white-hot."

Decker approached and shook my hand. "The timing is fuckin' crazy, but the announcement is a truly happy one."

"Thanks," I muttered, smiling when Siren put her arm through Deck's.

"When you tell this story, Ashford, and I know you will, be sure to get it right. *I* was the one who proposed."

"I'll remind you two wacky lovebirds that we have a mission to wrap up."

"Smoke? Will you come with me?"

There was a knock at the door, and Hughes answered. When he closed it behind him, he had a box in his hand. "Is this what you're off after?"

Siren nodded.

"I had one of my guys swing by and get it since it seemed for a while we'd never get the two of you out of the bedroom." Hughes stepped closer and handed it to her.

"I don't have the key," she murmured.

"May I?"

She looked at me with scrunched eyes. "Sure."

I took the box from her hands, gripped the tiny padlock, and ripped it off.

"If that wasn't the sexiest thing ever," she murmured only loud enough for me to hear. "I feel like proposing all over again."

"Do you want some privacy?" I asked.

She shook her head. "Not from you."

"If you'll excuse us," I said to the others in the room as I led her down the hallway and back into the bedroom. She sat on the edge of the bed and rested both her hands on top of the box.

"I feel as though it holds the secret of life or something." She laughed. "Am I being too dramatic?"

I put my hand on top of hers. "Whatever is inside, is something your mother wanted you to have."

"But, Byrne. Why did he want it?"

"You heard him say that you're just like your father. Maybe you'll find what he meant."

"He did say that, didn't he?"

"Go ahead, Siren. Open it."

"Oh my God," she gasped, taking the contents out of the first envelope. "Guerin wasn't investigating the drug gangs as much as she was IMI." I waited as she continued reading. She gasped again and handed the paper to me, pointing at a name on the page. "Brendan O'Connor. That's my father."

I read what she had. "This says that your dad was part of the task force investigating corruption in Irish Military Intelligence."

"They had proof," she said, reading what was in the second envelope. "Guerin was working on an exposé at the time of her death. Several members of that task force were also killed the same week." Siren kept reading and then looked up at me. "But not all. According to this, there were other agents who went unidentified. Three are named here."

"That's what Byrne was after. Tying up loose ends."

Siren shook her head. "It's been twenty-six years. Why haven't they come forward?"

I skimmed that page when she handed it to me. I recognized one of the names—Pierre Martin, Collete and Emelie's father. "Because they're dead."

"If that's the case, why did Byrne want to get his hands on this?"

"Because he had no way of knowing whether anyone else was identified."

Siren and I slowly went through the contents of the box. There was nothing contained within it that pointed to Byrne, Antonov, or Kim working together or with the disgraced and imprisoned former CIA director.

It would be a blow to Cope when I informed Doc Butler of such. However, I knew the guy well enough to know there was no way he'd let this matter drop, and neither would Doc. We owed it to the agents who'd lost their lives protecting ours, to avenge their deaths by holding those responsible, accountable.

"What's that?" I asked when Siren pulled out a smaller envelope. Inside was a single folded piece of paper, and what was on it had been handwritten.

"My dearest Aileen," Siren began. "That was my mother's name." As she continued reading, tears fell from her eyes. "He loved her so much." Siren brushed away her tears and laughed. "Even though, most of the time, he wanted to wring her neck." She looked up at me. "Where have I heard that before?"

I watched the expressions on her face change as she continued to read, in awe. Not just of her beauty, but of her bravery and resilience, her tenacity, and her strength.

"His mother's name was Siobhan."

"Your grandmother."

*"My grandmother."*

# Epilogue

*Smoke*

"What do you think?" I asked as I watched Siren read through the two proposals she'd received.

"I've never worked with Doc Butler or anyone from the K19 team," she said.

"They're good people."

"Does that mean you'd rather work for them?"

I smiled and shook my head.

"I think, at the minimum, I should meet them." Siren's eyes opened wide, and she looked into mine. "Wait. Fatale is Doc's *wife*?"

"She is."

"I just got chills. God, she's incredible. I mean, I don't know of any female agent in the UK who didn't want to follow in her footsteps. Most of the men, too."

"She was one of MI6's best."

Siren turned her head and looked out the plane's window. "And yet, she gave it all up for love."

"MI6, yes, but she is K19's managing partner."

"It's so beautiful," Siren murmured, looking down at the mountain range I'd called home all my life. I leaned over and looked at the same view she was.

"No regrets about selling your house in Dublin?"

She turned and kissed me. "None."

I pointed to the papers she held in her hand. "They're both generous offers."

"Come on, Smoke. Just tell me who you want to work for. K19 Security Solutions or the Invincibles?"

"I told you, it's your decision."

"That's hardly fair." She folded her arms and pouted.

"We could always stay independent."

She tapped her lower lip. "We could do. But then, what if neither of them gives us any assignments?"

"I can think of plenty to fill our time."

"At the ranch?"

"Just in our bedroom."

"Will there be all-night vigilante rides when we get home?" she asked.

I cocked my head.

"The cattle rustlers."

"Thankfully, no. Decker's security system not only stopped them from getting on our ranch, but through the facial-recognition software built into it, there were enough arrests to take most of that group down."

"Were they from the area?"

I nodded. "One of the ring leaders was a guy I had a run-in with over the way he treated his horses."

"Ms. Wynona said that sometimes you had to do that—take them against the owner's will."

"I want you to understand that me forcing someone to give up animals that are being abused is completely different from someone stealing my cattle."

"I do understand that." Siren bit her bottom lip. "I have to confess I've never ridden a horse."

"That doesn't matter to me."

"Will you teach me?"

I ran my fingers through her hair that was still growing back.

"I don't want you to coddle me, Smoke. It'll drive me mad."

"I don't think I could stand it if anything ever happened to you."

"Nor I, you, but we can't live our lives with the constant worry of it."

I leaned my head against the seat and closed my eyes. "In sickness and in health, in stubbornness and submission…"

"*Submission?* If that's what's written into your vows, Smoke, I swear I'll—"

I grasped the back of her neck and kissed her long enough that I felt the muscles in her body go slack. She pulled back and rested her head on my shoulder.

"Do you think we've been unfair to Ms. Wynona and Zeke about having our wedding at the ranch? It's so much extra work."

"I've given them both free rein to hire as much help as they need."

"If you think Ms. Wynona will admit to needing help, *you're* mad."

I laughed. Once we were home, I had no doubt my sweet Siren would respectfully take charge and ensure Ms. Wynona had all the support she needed.

"I'm so happy Uncle Gene is coming to the wedding. He's the closest thing I have to family."

We both agreed not to have anyone stand up with us, although Gene would be walking Siren down the aisle, and I made arrangements for Hammer to marry us.

Neither of us had parents still living, nor siblings, and yet, with all of the agents and operatives we'd worked with, our combined guest list topped one hundred.

"You know everyone from the K19 team has responded that they'll be at our wedding. As have the Invincibles."

"I didn't think of that. Although I'll hardly be in interview mode on the most important day of my life."

I kissed her again, harder and deeper than I had a couple of minutes earlier.

"I know them all well, and there isn't a single person from either firm who will talk about business that day."

"Not even Rile?"

"Even if he tried, which I doubt he would, Kensington would intervene."

"I'm so happy they're together."

It was protecting Kensington that had brought Siren and I together—the same mission had come close to costing her life. There was a time I wondered if Rile could let go of his past enough to let Kensington into his life, but she hadn't given him much choice. I smiled at that, so thankful Siren would've done the same for us.

If I had tried to walk away, she would've followed. Had she been the one to test our love in that way, I may not have been as brave.

Siren wound her arm through mine, and I kissed her forehead.

"Look," she said, pointing out the window. "I can see the Blazing T!" She sighed and smiled. "I can't wait to be home."

In all the times I'd looked down at the same view as I flew back from missions around the world, I'd never felt the peace and contentment I heard in Siren's voice. Not until today. "I can't wait to be home either," I said, for the first time, meaning every word.

Keep reading for a sneak peek
at the next book
in the Invincibles Series,
HANDLED!

# 1

*Cope*

I took a deep breath, making sure there were no holes in the story I was about to tell. I had to sell it and sell it good because the people I was lying to were trained to recognize even the most minute mistruths.

If I failed to convince any one of them, the house of cards I'd carefully built would come tumbling down.

"You better be fucking sure you can protect me, Cope," the agent I'd handled since the beginning of both our careers said last night when I told him his arrest was scheduled for this morning.

"You've trusted me this far, don't blow it now by panicking."

"I'll be the one locked up in a cell like a goddamn sitting duck."

"Just keep your mouth shut and let me handle it like I always do. If you don't, every risk we've taken in the last seven years will be for nothing." I didn't need to add that if he talked, I'd fucking kill him.

# About the Author

*USA Today* and Amazon Top 15 Bestselling Author Heather Slade writes shamelessly sexy, edge-of-your seat romantic suspense.

She gave herself the gift of writing a book for her own birthday one year. Forty-plus books later (and counting), she's having the time of her life.

The women Slade writes are self-confident, strong, with wills of their own, and hearts as big as the Colorado sky. The men are sublimely sexy, seductive alphas who rise to the challenge of capturing the sweet soul of a woman whose heart they'll hold in the palm of their hand forever. Add in a couple of neck-snapping twists and turns, a page-turning mystery, and a swoon-worthy HEA, and you'll be holding one of her books in your hands.

She loves to hear from my readers. You can contact her at heather@heatherslade.com

To keep up with her latest news and releases, please visit her website at www.heatherslade.com to sign up for her newsletter.

# MORE FROM AUTHOR HEATHER SLADE

BUTLER RANCH
*Kade's Worth*
*Brodie's Promise*
*Maddox's Truce*
*Naughton's Secret*
*Mercer's Vow*
*Kade's Return*
*Butler Ranch Christmas*

WICKED WINEMAKERS
FIRST LABEL
*Brix's Bid*
*Ridge's Release*
*Press' Passion*
*Zin's Sins*
*Tryst's Temptation*

WICKED WINEMAKERS
SECOND LABEL
*Beau's Beloved*
Coming Soon:
*Cru's Crush*
*Bones' Bliss*
*Snapper's Seduction*
*Kick's Kiss*

ROARING FORK RANCH
Coming Soon:
*Roaring Fork Wrangler*
*Roaring Fork Roughstock*
*Roaring Fork Rockstar*
*Roaring Fork Rooker*
*Roaring Fork Bridger*

THE ROYAL AGENTS
OF MI6
*Make Me Shiver*
*Drive Me Wilder*
*Feel My Pinch*
*Chase My Shadow*
*Find My Angel*

K19 SECURITY
SOLUTIONS TEAM ONE
*Razor's Edge*
*Gunner's Redemption*
*Mistletoe's Magic*
*Mantis' Desire*
*Dutch's Salvation*

K19 SECURITY
SOLUTIONS TEAM TWO
*Striker's Choice*
*Monk's Fire*
*Halo's Oath*
*Tackle's Honor*
*Onyx's Awakening*

K19 SHADOW OPERATIONS
TEAM ONE
*Code Name: Ranger*
*Code Name: Diesel*
*Code Name: Wasp*
*Code Name: Cowboy*
*Code Name: Mayhem*

K19 ALLIED INTELLIGENCE
TEAM ONE
*Code Name: Ares*
*Code Name: Cayman*
*Code Name: Poseidon*
*Code Name: Zeppelin*
*Code Name: Magnet*

K19 ALLIED INTELLIGENCE
TEAM TWO
Coming Soon:
*Code Name: Puck*
*Code Name: Michelangelo*
*Code Name: Typhon*
*Code Name: Hornet*
*Code Name: Reaper*

PROTECTORS
UNDERCOVER
*Undercover Agent*
*Undercover Emissary*
Coming Soon:
*Undercover Savior*
*Undercover Infidel*
*Undercover Assassin*

THE INVINCIBLES
TEAM ONE
*Decked*
*Edged*
*Grinded*
*Riled*
*Smoked*

THE INVINCIBLES
TEAM TWO
*Bucked*
*Irished*
*Sainted*
*Hammered*
*Ripped*

THE UNSTOPPABLES
TEAM ONE
*Furied*
*Merried*

COWBOYS OF
CRESTED BUTTE
*A Cowboy Falls*
*A Cowboy's Dance*
*A Cowboy's Kiss*
*A Cowboy Stays*
*A Cowboy Wins*